ISBN: 9798764586144

Also by Stephen Taylor
The Danny Pearson Thriller Series

Amazon Author Page

A Short Time To Kill

The Danny Pearson Series Shorts 1 - 4

By
Stephen Taylor

Contents

SNIPE

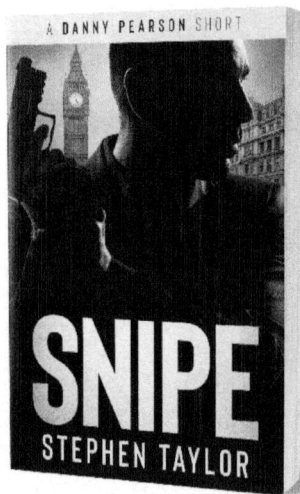

ONE

The old jewellery shop in Hatton Garden hadn't changed a bit. The last time Danny Pearson was there was when he was ten. When his dad retired after thirty-five years in an engineering factory, his workmates had a whip round and he wanted to buy a watch with it. He'd taken Danny with him and the two of them looked through the glass displays until he'd found one he liked. After his dad passed away, his mum handed the watch down to him. He smiled to himself nostalgically. It was weird; the smell of the place—all wood and polish—triggered the memory deep in his mind as if it was yesterday. Yep, still the same.

'Can I help you, sir?' said a grey-haired

assistant in his sixties.

'Yes, I've got this watch I'd like repaired,' said Danny taking in the old man. He couldn't be sure, but it was possible it was the same guy that sold it to his dad all those years ago.

'I can certainly have a look for you. Are you sure you want it repaired? It's not worth much; the repair will most likely cost more than it's worth.'

'I'm sure—sentimental value,' said Danny with a smile.

'Very good, sir, I'll just fill out a repair slip for you.'

Taking in the shop, Danny caught a glimpse of the reflection in a jewellery case. Three mopeds had pulled up outside. The pillion passengers all wore dark padded jackets, one-way black visors on their crash helmets. The hairs on the back of Danny's neck stood up as they turned to the shop. Each one had a hand on something bulky under their jackets.

The shop's too small, not much room to move.

'Call the police. You're about to get robbed,' said Danny, his face hardening, his muscles tense, ready.

The old man took one look at his face and shrank back into the stockroom with his phone. The three passengers burst into the shop, all noise and distraction as two of them swung baseball bats around. That didn't bother Danny much; the third was wielding a sawn-off shotgun—that did bother him.

'Don't fucking move! Get over there,' he shouted from behind his helmet.

'Which is it?' said Danny unimpressed, his dark brown eyes tracking all three of them, assessing options.

'Huh, what? Shut up and move,' he said, pointing to the corner with the shotgun.

Behind him the other bikers were breaking the glass cabinets with their baseball bats, whooping and laughing as they scooped out the jewellery into rucksacks. One came over to the counter and picked up Danny's father's watch, throwing it into his rucksack without a second glance. Danny ground his teeth as his eyes narrowed. The muscles in his legs and shoulders tensed, ready to move.

It happened in a heartbeat. A rider banged on the glass to hurry them up. Taking his eyes off

Danny, the gunman turned his helmet to look. Danny dipped under the line of fire and grabbed the barrel of the shotgun. With his full bodyweight behind it, he jabbed the butt of the gun into the guy's ribs. He went down like a sack of spuds, clutching his side, a muffled wheezing emanating through the helmet.

With two hands on the gun barrel, Danny sideswiped another helmeted thief. It connected hard, cracking the helmet and ripping the visor off. The blow knocked his skinny build clean off his feet, sending his head into the wall on the other side. He bounced off it like a pinball, ending up in a heap on the floor.

Spinning round, Danny caught sight of the one with his watch flying out the door. Dropping the shotgun Danny headed after him. With the revs screaming, the pillion threw the rucksack on his back and leaped on the back. The driver took off with his buddy holding on to him, and the second moped following close behind. The guy on the third moped wasn't as quick. Flustered, he crunched the gears, lurching it forward. Danny grabbed his helmet under the chin as he passed, pulling him clean off the bike as he threw him into the jewellers' doorway like a ragdoll.

Pulling the moped upright, Danny hopped on and screamed off after the bikes ahead. The chase wasn't exactly high speed; the mopeds were the thieves' vehicle of choice because they could easily escape police cars in London's heavily congested traffic. With the moped he was after weighed down with two people, Danny started gaining on them. He pulled alongside the solo rider and watched his helmet turn as he looked over expecting his buddy. Panicking he tried to kick out and knock Danny away. Swerving into the bus lane Danny turned and smiled back, pointing his finger forward. Following its direction, his helmet turned to see the brake lights of a Transit van in front of him. As Danny passed the van on the inside, he heard a loud metallic thud behind him. Weaving his way in between the traffic, he came up behind the other bike as it bumped up the curb and headed across a park. He followed in the wake of mothers screaming as they grabbed their toddlers and scrambled out of the way.

Coming alongside the other bike, Danny

dived across, crashing all three of them onto the soft grass. Scrambling to their feet, the thieves tried to run for it. He let the rider go, and grabbing the passenger with the rucksack, he hammered him to the ground. Pulling off the helmet with his fist drawn back, he stopped in surprise—the boy looked about twelve. He looked back at Danny, his lip starting to tremble and tears streaming from his eyes.

Oh, for Christ's sake!

'What's your name?'

'Keanu Wicks. Don't hurt me, mister. I'm sorry,' he said snivelling.

'How old are you?'

'Thirteen.'

Danny shook his head. Grabbing the rucksack he stood up.

'Go home and explain to your parents why they should expect a visit from the police,' he said brushing grass out of his unruly mop of dark hair. Leaving the boy, he turned and headed back the way he came. Ignoring the sound of sirens, Danny ducked under the police tape and headed for the door of the Hatton Garden jewellers. Walking through the police cars, he glanced at the gang gloomily sitting handcuffed in the back. Without their helmets he could see they were all young—teenagers, a couple early-twenties at most. Danny pushed past two officers on the door and dumped the rucksack on the counter. Looking at the old man, he pulled his father's watch out of the bag and handed it to him.

'One watch for repair,' he said, as the policeman grabbed his shoulder trying to get his attention.

'It would be a pleasure, sir,' said the old man with a smile.

TWO

A prison transport vehicle pulled into the yard of the review board building. As the metal gates shut behind it, four officers moved to the rear doors. Two moved in and stood either side of the little transport cell. With a clink of the heavy lock, they opened the door right back, tensing apprehensively at the muscular monster wedged and chained on the seat inside.

'Come on, Snipe, let's be having you.'

He stood slowly and shuffled through the cell door, rattling in chains from his wrists to his ankles. The guards got ready to help him down at the edge of the steps. Instead, Snipe jumped to the ground, making all four officers flinch as he landed solidly between them. A wide grin spread across his bearded face, his intense blue eyes burning in a defiant stare. Regaining their composure, the transport team escorted him to a heavy metal door and handed him over to the guards of the building. The transport team watched as they took charge and led him inside, shutting the door behind them.

'Bloody review board. That's a joke. God help us if that lunatic ever gets out.'

***

The guards removed Snipe's chains in a holding area before leading him into a large oak-panelled room. At the far end sat the review board behind a long table. The four of them flicked through files and case notes without so much as a glance Snipe's way. The guards showed him to a solitary chair in the middle of the room where he sat arms crossed, motionless, staring at the board.

'Good morning, er, Terrence, isn't it?' said a chubby middle-aged woman looking at him over her glasses, her long grey hair tied up in an old-fashioned bun on top of her head.

'My friends call me Terry,' Snipe said in a low gravelly voice.

'Right, Terry. As you know, we are here to review your eligibility for parole. Your case file says that since the incident at Broadmoor two years ago, you've been behaving yourself and have responded well to prescribed medication and psychological counselling. Tell me, Terry, how do you feel about the pain and suffering you've caused in the past?'

'Listen, lady, I'm sorry for the people I've hurt, my head wasn't right. I'm in a better place now and just want to be a useful member of society again,' Snipe said, his unblinking stare never leaving her.

'Mmm, that's very admirable, Mr Snipe, but I'd like to delve a little deeper if I may,' said a studious-looking man in a tweed suit and bow tie.

'And who might you be?' growled Snipe, turning his attention and intensity onto the new speaker.

'Dr Francis Pike. I'm here to assess your current state of mind,' he said, pausing for effect and any reaction from Snipe. When he got none he continued.

'I'd like to know how you feel about the events that led to your brother, Nicholas's death?'

Snipe resisted reacting but his face hardened and his nostrils flared.

'My brother and I have—had—the same condition. I have help and medication. He didn't. His death was unfortunate, but it was his own doing,' said Snipe softly, without emotion.

'I'm glad to hear it. Quite a change for someone who only two years ago nearly killed three guards while trying to escape, and what was the reason for trying to escape? Ah yes, to kill the man who killed your brother. Daniel Pearson, a military hero who killed your insane brother in self-defence,' Pike said, leaning forward in his seat, a smug look on his face as he goaded Snipe.

Snipe's muscular frame tensed, the veins in his neck raised as he gritted his teeth.

'It wasn't his fault, Pearson was to blame,' he said leaning forward menacingly, a darkness coming over him.

The board leaned back apprehensively, apart from Pike who wanted to push Snipe further to prove he was unfit for parole.

'No, Mr Snipe, your brother was a lunatic and was responsible for a string of murders across several countries. It is my honest opinion that if I granted you parole, a similar course of events would—'

Snipe launched himself forward with incredible speed for a man of his size. He grabbed either side of Pike's head and snapped his neck in one swift twist. He sideswiped the skinny man sitting next to Pike, the blow from his hammer-like fist dropping him to the floor. With the fury in his face vanishing as quickly as it came, he turned to the chubby middle-aged woman on the end of the table.

'Have you got a car?' he said smiling politely.

'Y-yes, here take it. Just don't hurt me,' she said, pulling her keys out of her bag with shaking hands.

'What is it?'

'I, er, it's a Fiat 500,' she said, crying with fear.

'I'm not getting away in a fucking Fiat 500,' Snipe growled, grabbing her by the bun on top of her head and ramming her face into the table. It hit with such force that her bloody face bounced off backwards to land her flat on her back, whimpering on the floor. Turning his attention to the youngest member of the board, Snipe took in the expensive suit and good haircut.

'And what car have you got?' he said leaning in, an insane look in his eyes.

'It's an M5, I've got a BMW M5,' he said as fast as he could.

'Give it up, Snipe,' came a shout as the two guards ran in through the door.

Snipe rolled his eyes.

'Don't go anywhere. I'll be right back,' he said to the suited guy before turning slowly to face the guards.

Straightened up, he tensed and flexed, cracking his neck from side to side as his body physically seemed to grow in size. With his head tilted forward slightly, his eyes looked up at them with hate and menace and insanity.

'Take it easy, Snipe, don't make things worse for yourself, okay? Just get down on your knees with your hands behind your head.'

The guards stood apart with their taser guns levelled at Snipe. He went for them without a second thought, causing them to fire in unison. The charges went off, sending the little barbs with wires attached whipping through the air, catching Snipe in the chest. The air crackled as thousands of volts surged through Snipe's body. He slowed to a halt for a second or two before his veins bulged and face flushed with rage and he kept on coming.

'Y—you'll have t—to do better th—than that,' he grunted through the pain. Grabbing the wires, he pulled the barbs out of his chest. Throwing them aside, he picked the chair up and broke it over one guard's head. The other one started hitting Snipe with his baton. The blows on the back of his head and shoulders just bounced off. Snipe spun round and grabbed the guard's wrist with one hand and his throat with the other, lifting him until his feet were off the ground. Staring at him intently he squeezed, the officer pummelling Snipe's arms an effort to free himself. Snipe started to grin, the pleasure clear in his face as the man passed out, hanging limply in his grip. Dropping him on the floor, Snipe shut the door and started pulling the clothes off the largest one. When he'd squeezed into the ill-fitting uniform, he turned the door entry cards over in his hand and looked to the suit with the BMW M5.

'Come on, twinkle toes, let's go for a drive,' he said, putting the guard's hat on with the peak pulled down low.

THREE

After the excitement of the day before and the hours of the night before at the police station giving statements, Danny was glad he had a fairly quiet day ahead of him. He pulled into his underground parking space. Avoiding the lift as he always did, he made his way up the stairs to the offices of Greenwood Security. He said good morning to Lucy on reception and made his way to his office, next to his friend and owner of the company, Paul Greenwood.

'Morning, Paul,' he said, poking his head around the door.

'Danny, quick, come and see this,' Paul said urgently.

When he went in, Paul was pointing at the TV

with the remote while turning it up.

'Terrence Snipe escaped while attending a parole hearing yesterday. The inmate from Broadmoor high security hospital killed four people before escaping disguised as a prison guard, with a member of the parole board as a hostage. He got away in the hostage's car, which was later found abandoned in Battersea, with the body of the owner in its boot. The man had been beaten to death with a prison guard's baton.'

A mug shot flashed up on screen, Terrence Snipe's face projecting itself out of the screen.

'The police have advised not to approach Mr Snipe, who is considered extremely dangerous. If anyone has seen, or has information regarding Mr Snipe's whereabouts, please contact Crimebusters at the number below.'

'Christ, even with the beard and long hair he looks just like him,' said Paul, turning the TV off.

'I didn't know he had a brother,' said Danny with growing unease.

'I'll phone Jenkins at MI6, see what he can find out. Just as a precaution, is Trisha still at her mum's?'

'Eh, yeah, she's there for a few more days,' said Danny, thinking about his girlfriend.

'And your brother?'

'In Tenerife with Tina.'

'Good. Better safe than sorry. I'll let you know what Jenkins says.'

Danny went to his office and sat back, thinking about Terrence's brother, Nicholas Snipe. They'd met in the SAS when Snipe was assigned to Danny's team. During the following few missions it became clear Snipe's growing hate for Danny as team leader, and his lust for killing was getting out of hand. It came to a head when Snipe killed an innocent villager in Iraq before raping and strangling his wife. He'd got away with it because it was a war zone and there was a lack of proof. They discharged him shortly afterwards, after finding him psychologically unstable. Snipe always blamed Danny for his discharge and threatened revenge. Their paths crossed again when Danny was working with Edward Jenkins and Paul for MI6; they were trying to stop a cyber-attack by a terrorist group called The Faith. Snipe was working for the leader, Marcus Tenby, as one of his paid killers. When the plot failed, Snipe came after Danny and tried to kill him. The fight went Danny's way, and he killed Snipe in self-defence.

Paul knocked on the open door, bringing him back to the present day.

'Just been on the phone to Jenkins. Not good news, I'm afraid. One of the board members, Mrs Bramley, has just come out of surgery; several facial fractures and a destroyed nose. She's made a statement. Apparently it all went pear-shaped when a Dr Francis Pike pushed him about his brother's death. Snipe brought your name up as the one to blame, before, well, you know the rest.'

'Great, why is it all the nutters hold grudges?'

'I don't know. Anyway, the police are sending a DI round to talk to you, and a couple of officers for protection,' said Paul, smirking at the thought of the police trying to protect Danny.

'What? Can today get any worse? And you can take that bloody smile off your face.'

FOUR

Snipe's mind wandered as he looked up at the four-storey block of ex-authority flats in Shadwell, East London. These days they were all privately owned, sold off by the council years ago. Number 46 on the top floor had been the Snipe family home for him, his brother, Nicholas, and their alcoholic, abusive father. Their mother had died when they were at primary school and their father had thrown all his blame and hate onto the two boys. When he was old enough and big enough, Terrence had strangled him slowly while his brother had watched. He'd gone to prison while Nicholas went into care and then into the army. They'd kept in contact, sharing an understanding; a bond no one else understood. Then Pearson killed him. He tensed and flexed, his mind clouding with violent thoughts. He stood for five minutes just staring out from under a hoodie he'd stolen off a washing line. When the red mist lifted and his thoughts came under control, he moved towards the stairwell. On the top floor he paused outside number 46, ghosts from his past screaming in his head. Shaking it off he knocked on the door. A stocky twenty-something man answered.

'Yeah, what do you want?'

'Avon calling,' said Snipe, chuckling.

'What? Piss off,' the man replied swinging the door to slam it.

Snipe's hand slammed on it, pushing it back open.

'Did you know that if you punch someone hard enough in the Adam's apple you can kill them?' said Snipe with a low growl, his eyes twinkling excitedly.

'Look, just fuck off or I'm calling the pol—'

The blow to his throat came with such ferocity and speed it sent him sliding back along the hall like a ragdoll. He lay there clutching his throat, panicked horror on his face as he desperately tried to get air past his crushed windpipe. Stepping into the flat Snipe closed the door casually behind him. The man's lips were turning blue as he hissed and gurgled and started to convulse. Snipe stepped over him and walked into the kitchen. The fittings had all changed but the layout was the same. He opened the door to the larder cupboard and started throwing the hoover, mop and bucket out of his way. Tapping the wall until he heard the hollow sound he was looking for, he stood up and kicked a hole through the soft plasterboard. Reaching in he pulled out a cloth sack and opened it. With a smile he pulled out a Glock 18 automatic pistol and tucked it in the back of his trousers. He reached in the bag again and pulled out a large wad of fifty-pound notes and a fake passport. Opening it he looked at his brother's picture with his short crew cut and clean-shaven face.

'Thanks, little brother. Time to settle the score.' He put the money in his pocket and looked at his brother's photo while running his fingers through his beard.

'Mmm, a shave and a haircut and we'd look pretty much identical.'

'Craig, what's all the noise about? I'm trying to sleep. You know I've got another shift tonight,' came a shout from the bedroom.

Snipe cocked his head towards the sound, a grin creeping across his face and his eyes twinkling with menacing excitement.

'Sorry dear,' he said in a whisper. Turning he walked towards the bedroom.

'Craig, are you there?'

FIVE

Looking down from his office Danny watched the police car draw up below. Following the police car was a familiar tatty blue Mini. He watched an attractive woman step out, tall and slim in a tailored blue trouser suit, her shiny brown hair swishing in a ponytail that exposed her dark Moroccan features. Danny smiled to himself. He hadn't seen Nichola Swan since his tangle with the Russian Mafia a few years back. They'd had a brief affair; bad timing—it didn't last long. Moving away from the window he walked to reception to meet them. The lift door opened and Nichola Swan walked out with a police officer. He waited outside while she came in. Seeing Danny she smiled with a row of perfect white teeth.

'Mr Pearson, how lovely to see you again,' she said, keeping it formal in front of Lucy, the receptionist.

'DCI Swan, lovely to see you, too,' he said with a smile.

'It's DC Nichola Swan now,' she said, flashing her badge.

'Congratulations. Is Billy no-mates out there coming in?'

'Danny—be nice. Have you got somewhere we can talk?' she said, turning serious.

'Eh, yes, come to my office,' he said leading the way.

He shut the door as she sat. Flipping open her leather satchel she pulled out a folder.

'It's good to see you again. After the Volkov thing I thought they'd lock you up for good,' she said, opening the folder and handing some papers to Danny.

'Just lucky, I guess. What's all this?'

'That is a psychological report on Terrence Snipe and some photos you should take a look at.'

Danny read through the report.

""'Terrence Snipe displays acute psychopathic tendencies, mixed with a high IQ of 155, and schizophrenia, although the medication is keeping him compliant. He should be handled with extreme caution."'

Danny put the report down and looked at the two pictures. The first one was of the bodies of the parole board room. The other was of a cell, presumably Snipe's. He'd covered the walls from head to toe in writing, scraped into the plaster.

Pearson must die. Kill Danny Pearson. Bastard Pearson.

The list went on, but he could sense a theme.

'Yep, he really likes you,' she said sarcastically.

'And you think Bill and Ben out there are gonna protect me better than I can protect myself. What's the point, Nichola?'

'The point is we have a van full of armed tactical police parked down the street. The pressure's on to get Snipe back behind bars before he kills again,' she said, putting the papers back in the folder.

'So you want to use me as bait?' he said, his dark eyes fixed on hers.

'Well, yes. But if he comes after you, surely it's better to have backup.'

'So, what's the plan?'

SIX

Sitting in the barber's chair, Snipe stared mesmerised at his own reflection. The beard had gone and the barber was busy with the clippers, shaving his long wavy hair into an extra short crew cut. With every strip of hair that fell from his head Snipe could see more and more of his little brother. The theme tune to the ITV News broke his concentration. Looking in the mirror he could see its backwards image on the waiting room TV. His gaze intensified as a message came on-screen.

'Escaped prisoner still at large.'

The blurb went on in the background: dangerous, murderer, mental issues. Snipe started to lose interest until a picture of Danny

Pearson exiting a house with two police officers appeared.

'Man helping police in locating the escaped prisoner,' said the newsreader as Snipe watched.

His anger started to build as he watched, grinding his teeth. The camera panned round to follow Danny walking past a street sign. Conrad Street. Snipe grinned. The screen went to a mugshot of himself with a Crimestoppers number underneath. Noticing the clippers had stopped touching his head, Snipe's eyes flicked up in the mirror. The barber was looking at the TV in the reflection. His eyes moved nervously down; he flinched and went pale when they met Snipe's. In a second Snipe exploded upright in a cloud of cut hair. Spinning around he picked up the barber's cut-throat razor and sliced through his carotid artery. A fountain of blood sprayed across the front window. The barber clutched desperately at his throat before losing conciousness and dropping to the floor. The shocked barber by the next chair froze to the spot, horrified. Snipe grabbed some scissors from the side. Moving at incredible speed he punched them repeatedly into the man's chest like a boxer with a winning combination. The second man dropped dead to the ground next to his colleague. Snipe turned to face the customer still sitting in the chair. Paralysed with fear he could only watch as Snipe stood behind his chair, spinning the bloody scissors in his hand, chuckling.

'Short back and sides, sir?'

SEVEN

The police moved around as Danny lounged on a beaten-up old sofa. DC Nichola Swan was in the middle of the room giving orders. When she'd finished she looked over at him.

'So, whose house is this, then?' he said looking at the peeling wallpaper.

'It's a safe house.'

'Hmm, not anymore,' Danny said with a half-smile.

'Well, it's worth a shot. We've got the news clip running on all networks. If he's as smart as they say, he'll get it.'

'Okay, so if he bites, how's this going to play out?'

'The tactical guys are in a van down the street,

two officers are upstairs and I'll be watching with two more from the house across the street.'

'And what do I do?' Danny said, his arms wide.

'Nothing. Just sit there, drink tea and look pretty,' she said, walking out the door.

Danny sat back and dug the TV remote out from the side of the sofa. He clicked it on. The old tube set took a few seconds to spring to life, only to hiss and crackle into a pictureless snowstorm. He tried a few more channels with the same result. Turning it off he threw the remote down and sat there staring at the walls of the depressing room.

EIGHT

Walking into the Apple store in Covent Garden, Snipe made a beeline for the laptops on display. Two kids were playing games while their dad got his iPad fixed at the Genius Bar. Walking up behind them Snipe then stood there motionless. It took a few seconds before one of the engrossed boys noticed his presence. He turned and looked up past the bloodstains on Snipe's hoodie top, eventually meeting a wide grin and intense blue, staring eyes peering out from under the hood.

'Fuck off,' growled Snipe, leaning in at the terrified child.

The two boys jumped and ran away to their father. Snipe chuckled and ran his bloodstained fingers over the keyboard. He searched Conrad Street and got three answers. Flicking through each one he searched them on Streetmap until he found the picture of the house from the news report.

'Gotcha,' Snipe said to himself.

'Excuse me, did you just swear at my son?' said the father, standing tall and puffing out his chest as his confidence waned, unnerved as the size and state of Snipe sunk in.

Snipe moved his head round slowly on his thick muscular neck.

Floppy hair, expensive jacket… fucking posh twat.

'You know, these laptops are exceptionally well made,' Snipe said in his best toff accent.

'What? I really think you owe my son an apology, don't y—'

Snipe closed the laptop while he was talking and gripped it with both hands. In one lightning move he powered the laptop up into the man's face, knocking him back over the phone display counter. He continued to batter him with the laptop as his kids screamed and cried. When bits started flying off and the man slid to the floor in an unconscious heap, Snipe placed the laptop gently back on its display and opened its bent lid up.

'Hmm, not as well made as I thought.'

Turning, he walked out and disappeared into the crowds of shoppers, tourists and workers going about their business in Covent Garden. Ducking down the steps Snipe made his way into the Tube station. He stood at a large board and studied the multi-coloured rings and lines that made up the Underground map. Tracing his finger down the London overground route, he stopped and tapped when he got to Crystal Palace. Turning, he went for the ticket machine.

I'm coming for you, Pearson.

NINE

Making his way along Albion Street, Snipe counted the houses until he got to the thirty-fourth one. Without hesitation he charged the front door, putting his boot and moving mass into a colossal impact of kinetic energy. The door blew inwards in a shower of splinters and bits of door frame. He moved through the house without caring if anyone was in. Reaching the back door, he flicked the latch and left. At the end of the garden he peeped over the fence. With nobody in sight, Snipe pulled himself over and dropped into the back garden of the house in the next street. He moved carefully to the back door, checking through the glass panels first before trying the handle, it was unlocked.

Slipping inside he stood in the kitchen, still and silent, listening. At the sound of movement upstairs he pulled a carving knife out of the block on the worktop. After taking a second to look at his new haircut in the reflection on the blade, he climbed the stairs, a wide grin spreading across his face.

'Ma'am, is that you? The cars are on their way. Three minutes,' came a voice from the room at the front.

***

The sound of radio talk and footsteps on the stairs woke Danny from his snooze. Nichola came in with the phone glued to her ear. Outside, police cars appeared and police piled in. She finished on the phone and looked at him, her face pale and a worried crease in her forehead.

'Snipe's surfaced. He went berserk in a barber shop near Leicester Square; killed two and cut the ears off a customer. Half an hour later he battered a man in the Apple store at Covent Garden. We've closed the area down and I'm taking the armed unit down there now. He can't have gone far,' she said, moving for the door as sirens wailed and a car took off at speed outside.

'I'll come with you,' said Danny, up off the sofa and moving towards her. She stood blocking the door with her hand out to stop him.

'Not this time, sorry, Danny. Just sit tight, I'll be back when we have something. Okay, I've left two officers in a car outside, there's one upstairs and one in the house opposite.'

'Ah, come on,' said Danny, bored and frustrated.

'No. Just stay here,' she said firmly. She held his gaze to make her point then left the house, tearing off in the second police car.

Danny slumped back down agitated. Sitting around waiting wasn't his style.

***

Looking through the net curtains of the upstairs bedroom, Snipe listened to the police radio and watched the police cars leave. The raspy wheeze from behind distracted him for a moment. He turned to see the police officer trying to drag himself towards the door, the carving knife sticking out between his shoulder blades.

'Hey, buddy, you leaving so soon?' Snipe said with a chuckle. He stood up and towered over him. Lifting his leg he placed the sole of his boot on the handle of the knife. The officer shook in pain, his arms twisting hopelessly, trying to reach behind him. Snipe eventually pushed so hard the blade exited his chest, digging into the floorboards beneath him. When he went limp Snipe stood still, staring down at him. His face was a vision of madness, eyes glinting and excited at his victim's last tremblings of life.

The moment was gone. Snipe's expression went passive and he returned to the window. He watched the police car on the road and the safe house opposite.

TEN

With its historic market in the centre of boutiques, trendy cafes, restaurants, and surrounding theatres, Covent Garden, one of London's biggest tourist attractions—was eerily quiet. Vans and police cars blocked all the access roads in and out. Armed police and beat officers checked the crowd against Snipes description as they rushed to leave the area. Panic set in as people pushed, fuelled by rumours of bombs and terrorist attacks, speculation twisting the truth like Chinese whispers working their way down the line. When the crowds eventually thinned, the police moved inwards, checking shops, bars, theatres and alleyways. By the market building, a police officer held the car door open for DC Swan. She entered the Apple store and introduced herself to the shop manager and tearful shop assistant. Moving into the back office she joined a colleague as he shuffled through the shop's CCTV.

'Hiya, Trevor, what have we got?'

'Morning, Ma'am, just a sec, I'll scroll it back for you,' he said clicking through the menus until the full screen image appeared showing Snipe as he entered the shop. The video of Snipe's hooded figure was terrifying. With his head down he moved confidently to the laptop displays like something wild, full of muscular menace. She watched him chuckle as he scared the kids away, then he started typing on the laptop. She couldn't see the screen from the angle of the camera. With her eyes glued to the footage, she jumped. The speed and ferocity of Snipe's attack on the father shocked her. She watched him place the bent laptop back down and open it up. As he turned to leave he tilted his head up at the camera, giving it a wide grin. Nichola turned to the shop manager.

'I need to know what he was looking at,' she

said, going back out to the shop floor.

The manager tapped on the few keys still left intact. The screen blinked a star-fractured picture back at him.

'Hold on a sec, it's still powered up,' he said taking it over to a monitor. He plugged a keyboard into the USB port and then attached a monitor. Google Street Map and the house on Conrad Street filled the screen.

'Shit! All units proceed immediately to 91 Conrad Street. Suspect is heading for the safe house. I repeat, suspect is heading to the safe house on Conrad Street,' she said, running for the door. Sirens echoed from neighbouring roads as police cars sped away from Covent Garden.

'Let's go, quick, go, go,' she said impatiently as she climbed in the back of her police car.

ELEVEN

Bored with staring at the walls, Danny walked through the open-plan room into the kitchen. He found some milk in the fridge that passed the sniff test and clicked on the kettle. After rummaging through the cupboards he found the coffee. As he stood pouring the hot water he heard gunshots. He rushed towards the living room window, only to slide to a halt and dive backwards over the sofa. At the same time, the police car from outside powered through the front in an explosion of bricks and glass and wood. Crouching, Danny couldn't see inside the car; the airbags had deployed, filling its windows as it kept coming. It smashed to a halt when it hit the fireplace, ripping the gas fire clean off the wall.

Danny stood upright as Snipe climbed out of the car. Their eyes locked. Snipe flexed and tensed, a carbon copy of his brother, the same stare full of murderous insanity. Danny stared back with unintimidated steely determination. Pulling the gun from behind his back, Snipe levelled it on Danny. He was so focused on his target he didn't see the police officer run in. He cracked Snipe's wrist with his baton, sending the gun clattering to the ground and sliding out of sight somewhere under the car. With a rage beyond reason, Snipe grabbed his wrist and headbutted him to the floor with terrific force. The officer went down in a heap, out cold.

Danny was already on the move. He charged forward and leapt off the sofa, landing a flying punch to Snipe's head. The blow should have put the man out, but Snipe just rocked back against the side of the car. Following it up, Danny let rip a combination of punches to the body and face. Danny followed his own combat advice—when you get the upper hand in a fight, attack and keep attacking until he ain't coming back at you.

From nowhere Snipe's insane rage kicked in. He surged forward, hammering blows with relentless fury. Danny blocked and tried to counter, but the blows kept coming, pushing him painfully back towards the kitchen.

I've gotta get on top of this.

Grabbing the toaster off the side, he whipped it around, ripping the plug out of its socket. It connected with the side of Snipe's head, knocking him sideways. He tried to swipe him again but got a boot in his stomach, kicking him backwards over the kitchen table on to the floor. Winded, Danny sucked in air, only to cough and get a heavy smell of gas leaking out from where the gas fire had been.

From the floor, the sight of Snipe's legs coming round the table prompted Danny into action. Coiled like a spring he pushed upwards, grabbing Snipe around the waist and lifting him off the ground. Charging forward he hurled Snipe over the sofa, sending him thudding into the car in the living room. Backing into the kitchen while Snipe dragged himself upright, Danny ripped the drawers open, looking for a weapon. Finding a potato peeler and bread knife, he turned, tensed and waited for Snipe to attack. His face red and the veins bulging with rage, Snipe started to move. A noise in the corner caught Danny's attention. The police officer was conscious and pointing his taser gun at Snipe.

'No, don't!' Danny yelled as the officer pulled the trigger.

The spark from the device ignited the gas in the room. A huge explosion of fiery energy flashed outwards from the centre. The blast wave blew Danny through the patio doors. He landed in the back garden in a shower of glassy shards. Sitting up, Danny looked through the inferno in the house. Mirroring him beside the back end of the car out the front of the house sat Snipe. They both stood and stared at each other, the sound of sirens ringing their approach in the distance.

Snipe tried to move forward to get at Danny, but the heat of the flames held him back. Insane and incensed, he roared, ripping his smouldering hoodie off, his muscles tense and veins popping as he roared again. As the sound of the approaching sirens finally registered, he backed away slowly, never losing eye contact until he disappeared out of sight.

Danny charged the fence to his right, kicking it into splinters. He tried the back door to the house next door but it was locked and too solid to force. Without stopping he crashed through another fence. This time they'd left the back door unlocked. He ran through to the front door, ignoring the screaming cleaner, and rushed out into the street. He spun around looking for Snipe but there was no sign of him. He spotted the officer laying by the front door and checked he was still breathing. After putting him into the recovery position, Danny checked his pockets for his phone. When he couldn't find it he looked into the flames and tried to remember where he had last seen it. With the sirens sounding close, Danny knelt down by the unconscious officer and pulled his phone out from his jacket pocket. Unlocking it with the officer's thumb print, Danny disabled the lock and pocketed it. Standing back up, he waited as police cars screeched into the street from either end.

TWELVE

In amongst the chaos of police teams and ambulance crews, DC Nichola Swan came over to Danny.

'I'm so sorry, it's my fault. I got the report and made a bad call pulling everyone off. God, three people have died. You could have died,' she said, tears welling up in her eyes.

'It's not your fault, it was the most logical choice,' said Danny only half-listening; other things were playing on his mind.

'Thanks. If you wait here, I'll get somewhere safe organised and a team to take you.'

Danny gave a nod of acknowledgement; something was nagging at him as he stared into the burning safe house.

She moved away to meet the coroner's private ambulance. After guiding them to pick up the three dead bodies, she organised an escort to take Danny to a new safe house.

'We're ready, ma'am, where's Mr Pearson?'

'Thanks, Davidson, he's over there by the—,' said Nichola stopping in surprise, first at the disappearance of Danny and then at the disappearance of the police car she'd left him by.

'Shit, Danny... Davidson, get onto Control and get me patched into car 103's radio.'

'Yes, ma'am,' he said, jumping on his comms.

Nichola looked up the road. She knew what Danny was capable of.

Where are you going?

THIRTEEN

Danny drove the police car towards central London. He pulled over when he was a couple of miles clear of the safe house. Pulling out the officer's phone, he made a call to Paul.

'Greenwood Security, how can I help you?' said Lucy, bright and bubbly as always.

'Hi, Lucy, is Paul in? It's Danny.'

'Sure, Danny, I'll put you through.'

The phone line played some light pop music until Paul came on.

'Danny! Are you okay? I've been following the reports from the barbers and Covent Garden.'

'Yeah, I'm fine. Look, I need you to do something for me,' Danny said, while checking for police cars in the mirror.

'What do you need?' said Paul, sensing the seriousness of the tone and getting straight to the point.

'Check the tracker in my works phone for me.'

'Why, don't you know where you are?' said Paul, joking as he tapped on his keyboard.

'Might be nothing, I've just got a bad feeling about something.'

'Okay, that sounds ominous. Right, according to this you're outside Scott's apartment.'

'Shit. Call Scott, tell him to stay away from his apartment. If he's there, tell him to get out, NOW. Call him, Paul, call him NOW,' said Danny hanging up. He jammed the car into gear and tore off towards Scott's apartment by the Thames.

He slid the car to a halt outside a tall, modern apartment building. Moving to the secure entrance, Danny tensed at the sight of the glassless door. He stepped through into the foyer and its sea of glass crystals glistening like diamonds around the concrete block that had recently gone through it. Like the entrance, the lift and stairs needed a fob to access them. Danny went to the stairs. Snipe had hammered the door with a fire extinguisher until it snapped in two. Fearing for Scott's life, Danny flew up the stairs three at a time. He powered on until he reached the top floor. He could see Scott's door ajar as he slid with his back against the corridor wall towards it. Standing silently for a minute or two, he listened. No sound. The apartment gave nothing away. Taking in deep breaths, Danny used his adrenaline and burst into the apartment. Keeping low and ready to move, he worked his way through the rooms. There was no sign of Scott or Snipe. He returned to the lounge. The ringing of a phone focused his attention on the coffee table. There in the middle, propped up against a coffee cup, sat his mobile, Scott Miller's number flashing insistently on its screen. Danny picked it up.

'Snipe.'

'Pearson, why don't you come and join us? I'd hurry if I were you, your friend is boring the arse off me. If he says old man one more time, I'm going to rip his throat out,' said Snipe in his usual low, menacing growl.

'Where?' said Danny bluntly. No emotion— he didn't want to give Snipe the satisfaction of knowing he'd rattled him.

'The Sky Garden, top of the Walkie Talkie. Alone. No filth.'

The phone went dead. Danny was on the move before Scott's face faded from the caller ID screen. He descended back down the stairs, this time a flight at a time as he jumped between landings. Thirty seconds from leaving the apartment, Danny was back in the police car and tearing off towards the iconic Walkie Talkie building at 20 Fenchurch Street. As he weaved his way around traffic, the radio burst into life.

'Danny, it's Nichola, what are you doing? You've gotta stop what you're doing and let us help you.'

'I can't do that, Nichola. I tried it your way and people died. Snipe's got my friend and I'm going to get him back.'

'Look, just stop where you are. We'll help you. We've got a GPS lock on the car; we're only five minutes away,' she said, genuine concern coming through in her voice.

'Sorry,' Danny said, pumping the accelerator even harder.

Several streets later the radio burst into life

again.

'All units, all units, proceed to 20 Fenchurch Street. A man armed with a knife has taken a hostage up to the Sky Garden. Armed officers are on their way.'

FOURTEEN

Within minutes Danny came sliding sideways onto Fenchurch Street. He obliterated a street sign as it bounced the car back into a straight line. Crowds running from the street entrance to the Sky Garden scattered for cover as he skidded to a halt outside. Seeing him exit from the police car, two security guards ushered him in.

'We've got nearly everyone down, officer. The guy's a lunatic! He's got a hostage and a bloody big carving knife. Er, where's the rest of you?' he said, noticing Danny's singed appearance.

'They'll be here any second. I was close by... er, gas explosion. Now move, I'm going up,' he said, dismissing the looks as he moved into the lift.

His stomach sank as the high-speed lift whizzed to the 37th floor. Just before the doors opened, Danny tensed. With one foot on the back wall he prepared to kick off and launch at Snipe. The doors slid open. A security guard ushered two crying Japanese tourists into the lift. Danny moved past them, turning to the guard as he went.

'Police. Do you know where he is?'

'He's up the steps on the top floor,' he said as the doors slid smoothly shut between them.

Edging out onto the lower level, Danny looked through the large hanger-shaped front window at the deserted outside terrace, with its panoramic views of central London. He knew the layout; he'd taken Trisha to the restaurant here on their first date. With no one in sight, he scooted over to the island-shaped coffee shop in the middle of the floor. Hopping over the counter, Danny rifled around for a weapon. When he couldn't find anything more deadly than a blunt cake knife, he hopped back over and made his way up the left-hand stairs which ran up past lush plants on one side and views across London on the other.

Looking around the open space near the top, Danny couldn't see any way of making a surprise attack. Snipe stood in the middle of the top floor, his back to the windows, and a good view of the left and right stairs that ran down either side of the Fenchurch restaurant. He had Scott in front of him, one hand firmly on his shoulder and the other pressing the carving knife lightly on his throat. He grinned at the sight of Danny, his eyes locking on with their unblinking intensity.

'Now the party can begin,' he growled.

'Scott, what did I teach you after the last time this happened?' he said ignoring Snipe.

Shaking, Scott lifted his head and looked at Danny. Even though he was scared stiff, Danny caught the look of understanding.

'What are you hiding behind him for, huh? Are you as big a coward as your brother?' shouted Danny, his eyes never leaving the knife.

Snipe's face went purple with rage and the knife flicked dangerously across Scott's skin, causing blood to trickle down his neck.

'You can watch matey here die for that, before I gut you like a fi—'

'NOW!' shouted Danny as Snipe pointed the knife towards him in a rage.

Scott dropped like a stone, elbowing back as hard as he could into Snipe's balls. As Snipe staggered back winded, Scott scooted off out of reach.

'Get out of here!' Danny yelled to Scott, who immediately made a break for the stairs. Charging forward Danny got to Snipe before he was steady enough to stab at him. Danny grabbed Snipe's wrist and twisted his tree trunk arm around with all his might. With a yell Snipe dropped the knife. Danny kicked it hard, sending it clattering down the stairs. His advantage didn't last long; Snipe recovered his balance and fought back with the power only an insane man could muster. He reigned down blow after blow. In the SAS Danny had been highly skilled in hand-to-hand combat, but the power and speed of Snipe's punches started finding their target and passed all Danny's attempts to block them.

With his head spinning, Danny crouched and kicked a heavy blow to the side of Snipe's knee. As it caved in Snipe went down on one side.

Jumping up, Danny drove his knee into Snipe's chin. The blow should have dropped an elephant but Snipe rolled as he fell back, flipping himself back upright. With a shake of his head he roared as he charged. Tackling Danny around the waist, he lifted him off the ground and kept on running, crashing them both through the glass doors of the Fenchurch restaurant. Shaking the glass off his head, Snipe slammed Danny down onto a dining table. Dazed and winded, Danny felt Snipe's hands gripping his neck like a vice. Already desperate for breath, stars and patterns danced in front of his eyes, partially blocking out the view of Snipe's insane grinning face.

Come on. Get out of this.

Spinning his arms around blindly behind him, he fumbled to grab a piece of cutlery as it slid past his touch. His vision started to fade as he danced on the edge of consciousness. With every ounce of strength he could muster, Danny punched both arms up, stabbing a fork into Snipe's left eye and shattering a wine glass into his right cheek. Screaming, Snipe staggered back before standing bolt upright, blood running down his face from glass on one side and the fork sticking out of his eye on the other. While staring at Danny he raised a trembling hand and grabbed the fork, pulling it out with a sickening spray of blood. Sucking in great gulps of air, Danny stood and backed towards the window overlooking the lower floor. He stood tense, readying himself for Snipe's next attack. He saw the rage building as Snipe physically seemed to grow as his muscles tensed.

Swing left and get him on his blind side.

Danny's fists clenched tighter as Snipe started to move. He took a couple of steps forward and stopped, looking left and right. Following his gaze Danny spotted the little red laser dots dancing in through the gallery window behind him.

'Armed police! Stay exactly where you are!'

Backing away from the marksmen's line of sight, Snipe moved back towards the restaurant door. He crunched across the glass before turning, his head swinging from side to side as he spotted something. With a smile spreading across his face, Snipe ripped a bench off its mount and charged the viewing window. Danny watched as Snipe hurled the bench through the window like a battering ram. He ran towards him in disbelief as the wind funnelled in through the open gap. Snipe turned. Little red dots from the police sights appeared on his chest. He looked defiantly at Danny before stepping back out the window and dropping out of sight. Danny ran forward grabbing the window frame so he could lean out, He looked down over the edge for Snipe's broken body 37 floors below.

FIFTEEN

To his surprise, he saw Snipe moving down the outside of the building in a window cleaner's cradle. He stopped four floors down and was busy bashing an office window with an iron bar. It imploded into a million pieces, letting the shouts and screams of the office workers out. Taking his jacket off, Danny looked at the police teams reaching the top of the stairs with DC Swan in the front.

'He's four floors down,' Danny shouted. Leaping out he grabbed the cables to the cradle with his jacket and slid down to the platform. Snipe was already halfway through the office as Danny jumped in. He heard him shouting as he pummelled a man in a grey suit.

'A fucking Smart car, what's wrong with you people?' he shouted as he grabbed another one.

'You better tell me you drive something good,' said Snipe, grabbing him by the throat.

'Please, I've got a Land Rover, don't hurt me.'

Snipe grabbed his building pass and car keys and pocketed them.

'Thanks,' he said with a grin, then headbutted the man to the ground.

'Come on, then,' Snipe roared at Danny across the office. Turning, he kicked the office door open and walked out into the foyer. Following him out, Danny came face-to-face with Snipe as he stood feet away in the lift. He was beckoning with his hands for Danny to enter, while staring madly with his one good eye.

'Come on, come on, come on,' he murmured repeatedly.

Not a lift, never get caught in a confined space. Kill box.

Hesitating, Danny could hear the police somewhere above, hammering their way down the stairwell. The lift dinged.

Fuck it.

'Aaargh!' shouted Danny as he charged through the closing doors.

As the high-speed lift hurtled its 30-second journey down, Snipe and Danny locked in a battle of punches, kicks, elbows and knees. The lift shaft boomed as they bounced each other off the sides. Although they were both tiring, Snipe's insanity-driven revenge and Danny's dogged determination kept them slugging it out. The lift doors opened as Snipe planted his boot in Danny's chest, kicking him clean out of the doors into the lower level car park. He slammed into the side of an AA breakdown van. The loud thud and rocking of the van caused an angry mechanic to yell from the other side.

'Oi, what the hell do you think you're playing at?'

Poking his head around the back, the sight of Snipe exiting the lift, one wide eye staring out from a wash of congealing blood, made him jump back out of sight again.

Danny ducked into the back of the van and pulled out a heavy torque wrench. As he turned his attention back to Snipe, something struck him round the head hard enough to knock him sideways. He raised the wrench instinctively to protect his head. The clang of metal on metal shook its way down his arm. As he got up, he looked forward in time to see the base of a fire extinguisher as it bashed off his face.

Falling to his knees, Danny fought to focus as stars danced in front of his eyes. Snipe raised the fire extinguisher again, bringing it down for another blow to Danny's head, the blow sent him to the floor but he hardly felt it, unconsciousness wasn't far away.

Lying on his back, Danny felt Snipe kneel on his chest. Snipe pulled the wrench from his hand and jammed it across his throat. With the world spinning, Danny felt as if he was outside his body, looking down at Snipe throttling someone else. Images floated through his mind: his dead wife and son, his brother, and friends Scott and Paul. Then came images of people he'd fought in the SAS and the bad guys after—the Volkov's, The Faith, and Snipe's brother, Nicholas. Then came pain and anger and the need to fight.

Like a bolt of lightning he was back in his body. His eyes shot open, and he grabbed

Snipe's face, sinking his thumbs into his damaged and good eyes. With new found adrenaline and anger pumping through his veins, he pushed until Snipe's eyeballs popped. Screaming, Snipe stood with the wrench still in his hand, and a constellation of red dots appeared on his chest.

'Armed police! Give it up, Snipe. Get down on your knees, hands behind your head.'

Snipe didn't move for ages. Eventually he cocked his head in Danny's general direction.

'I'll see you in hell,' he said. With a last grin he raised the wrench and roared, charging blindly toward the police. Gunshots echoed around the concrete as bullets ripped through his chest. He managed a few more steps before falling face-first onto the car park floor.

SIXTEEN

An ambulance drew up inside the cornered-off area. Danny sat in the back while a paramedic checked him over. Outside, DC Swan pushed her way through the sea of police and response teams. She climbed up the steps and sat down next to him.

'You okay?' she asked, a softness in her voice. It reminded him of a time when they had a different kind of relationship.

'I'll live,' he said giving her a half-smile.

'You once told me you have an annoying habit of doing that,' she said, putting her hand on his shoulder.

Danny started to laugh then quickly stopped when it made the side of his face hurt.

'I've gotta stop saying that. Am I under arrest?'

'What's the point? Some suit with a made-up name and no job title would only turn up and set you loose. Nah, assisting the police in their enquires sounds much better,' she said, climbing out of the ambulance.

'It was good seeing you again.'

'You too. Take care of yourself, Danny,' she said, a sadness in her eyes. Then she was gone.

'I say, let me through, old chap,' came the unmistakable sound of Scott from outside.

'That you, Scotty boy?' Danny said, raising his voice above the commotion.

Scott's face beamed around the ambulance door, his sandy-coloured hair bouncing around on his head.

'Come on, stop sitting there feeling sorry for yourself. I was the bloody hostage after all.'

Danny stood painfully and stepped down from the ambulance.

'You arsehole,' he chuckled, putting his arm around Scott to steady himself.

'Where's the nearest pub, Scott? You can buy me a pint for saving your life.'

'For your information, it was your fault I was kidnapped in the first place, and I saved my own life with my lethal fighting skills.'

Danny couldn't help laughing and wincing with pain at the same time.

'Okay, I give in. I'll buy the first round.'

Heavy Traffic

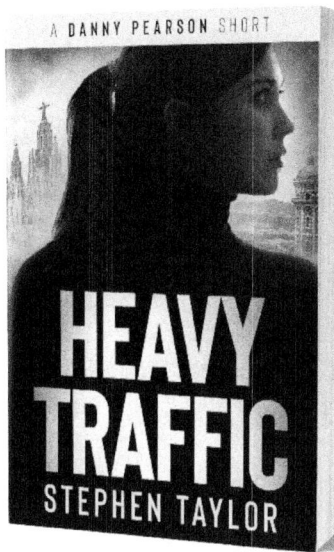

ONE

'How many more have you got to look at today, Scott?' said Danny to his best mate Scott Miller.

'Just one more, old boy. The house is just off the square at the top of this road. Why don't you park the hire car up and grab a drink while I go and view it,' said Scott pointing to a bar in the corner of the picturesque cobbled square.

'Sounds good to me, mate.'

Danny parked up and headed across to the bar with tables and umbrellas outside on the cobbles in the hot Spanish sunshine.

'I'll be about half an hour,' shouted Scott as he headed off down a side street in the direction of a traditional Spanish house that was for sale.

Ordering a beer, Danny sat down and took in

Altea's old town charm, with its white-washed buildings and narrow streets. He looked up at the bell tower of a pretty church on the other side of the square, its dark blue glazed roof tiles gleaming in the sunshine. Scott had decided it would be nice to have a holiday home in Spain and asked Danny if he fancied a few days in the sun. A trip with Scott was always fun, so Danny had readily agreed.

It was still early in the year and the town was fairly free of tourists. With its Mediterranean views and old town charm, Danny could see why Scott wanted a place here. He took a big gulp of ice-cold beer and relaxed in the warm spring sun. Movement in the street beyond their hire car caught his attention. A young woman was running. She kept turning her head to look behind her causing her long-disheveled hair to swish around in the breeze. He caught sight of her face, noting her wide eyes and frightened expression. Danny heard the squeal of skidding tyres on cobbles before he saw the black BMW speeding towards the running woman. Its passenger door already opening as it skidded to a halt beside her. A tall, skinny guy jumped out of the car and grabbed the girl. She shrieked, punching and kicking him as he dragged her to the back door. Angered by her struggling, the man punched her hard in the stomach, knocking the wind and fight out of her. Opening the rear door, he pulled her over to throw her across the back seat.

'I don't think the lady wants to go with you,' said Danny, walking towards the car.

'Mind your own business, this does not concern you,' said the man with a heavy accent, not Spanish—more Ukrainian or maybe Czech.

'Let go of her and she can decide for herself,' Danny said, his voice commanding and his face hard. His intense brown eyes remained focused on the man's every movement.

'Fuck off, English, I won't tell you again,' he said pushing the woman in the back of the car. He turned back and reached into his jacket.

Danny had already noticed the slight bulge of a firearm when the man stepped out of the vehicle. Moving at speed towards the car, he kicked the rear door as hard as he could, slamming it into the guy. Continuing the momentum, he stepped in and kept the door pushed shut with one hand, trapping the man between the door and the car body. With his other hand clenched into a fist, Danny powered a punch into the side of the skinny man's face. He flopped over the car roof. The gun, bits of paper and cigarettes flew out of his pocket onto the ground. Danny was about to move in and get the woman when a familiar click stopped him in his tracks.

'That's enough, tough guy. Move away or I shoot you right here.'

Danny looked across at the driver. He was out of the car and pointing a Beretta M9 handgun across the roof at his head. The guy was taller than the passenger, lean, with the same look of nationality. He had a scar across his jawline, turning near the ear and dropping down his neck. It stuck out prominently through his short, patchy, dark beard; the hair didn't grow on the scar tissue, so left a shiny pink line in the stubble. He held the gun level and steady at Danny's head, a tattoo visible between his thumb and forefinger of a dagger with a star behind it. Danny stepped reluctantly back. The guy had the look of someone who'd shot a gun before and the tattoo was rough and crude. Undoubtedly a gang tattoo earned in prison. The man Danny punched regained his composure. He picked up his gun and cigarettes and stood up, his anger clear on his face.

'I fucking kill this bastard,' he said slamming the car door.

Danny was running through options. He watched their eyes, waiting for the briefest lack of focus so he could duck, move or dive, or do anything to avoid a bullet in the head. His luck was in as the driver looked up to the square. The barman who'd served him was watching from the tables and a group of tourists was ambling around the square taking photos of the church.

'Aleksander, leave it. Get in,' ordered the driver, obviously in charge by the way he acted.

The passenger breathed heavily, obviously frustrated. A few seconds later he conceded and got back in the passenger seat. Danny noticed the same dagger and star tattoo on his hand.

Moving steadily, the driver backed up, keeping the gun and eyes on Danny until the last moment before ducking back in the car. He started it and screamed it away, snaking across the slippery cobbles. Danny watched it go, making a mental note of the licence plate as it went. As he turned back towards the bar he kicked something on the floor, it was a matchbook from Aleksander's pocket. Picking it up, he walked back to his table and sat down.

'Are you ok, my friend, you should be careful, very bad men, very bad,' the barman said putting another beer in front of Danny. 'Please have a drink on the house.'

'Do you know who they are?' said Danny, turning the matchbook over in his fingers.

'Albanians, they moved into the town last year. Drugs, extortion and I hear the trafficking of women.'

'What about the police?' said Danny reading the matchbook writing. Bar Apollo.

'They are very careful, no proof. The police do nothing,' the barman said, moving off to serve the tourists as they came in.

Danny drank his beer and stared at the address on the back of the matchbook. He pictured the woman's face, her eyes wide in terror.

Nope, I can't leave it.

Draining his glass, he went over to the barman.

'This guy is supposed to meet me here in a little while. Can you tell him I had to go somewhere and will meet him at the hotel later?' said Danny, showing him a picture of Scott and sliding him twenty euros.

'I will, thank you, señor.'

Danny left, crossed the square, and got in the small hire car. Turning it around on the cobbles he headed off towards the harbour.

Stephen Taylor

TWO

Danny drove down from the hilltop square towards the front. He hit the beach road where the bulk of the out of season holidaymakers congregated. They thinned out when he got to the edge of town and the harbor. Checking the satnav on his phone Danny parked up and got out. Opening the boot he pulled the carpeted board up, exposing the spare wheel. Reaching in, he grabbed the iron wrench by the car jack and tucked it into the back of his jeans. Slamming the boot shut he headed for Bar Apollo.

It didn't take long to find it, tucked in a side street off the harbour road. It definately wasn't a tourist bar, with its faded *Bar Apollo* sign looking tired on the peeling white-washed wall. Danny walked past on the opposite side of the street, checking out the empty plastic tables and chairs in front. Looking in through the open folding doors, he could see four men playing pool and a bored, scruffy old barman sitting behind the bar. Three of the men had the same look as the Albanian from the car: lean, sinewy, bordering on skinny, the same short dark hair and facial shape. The one with his back to Danny moved around the pool table. It was Aleksander from the square, a blackish-blue bruise blooming on the side of his face where Danny had hit him. The dagger and star tattoo was just visible as he slid the pool cue through his thumb and forefinger when he took aim. Danny moved out of sight and stood weighing up the options.

Leave it alone and walk away, or find the girl and help her?

It didn't take him long to decide.

'Fuck it,' he said, sliding the wrench out and heading across the road.

Aleksander and one other guy continued to play pool with their backs to Danny. The third guy stood at the bar ordering drinks. That left the fourth man on the far side of the pool table. He looked up, only partly interested in Danny's approach. His expression turned to one of surprise and apprehension as he watched the solid features, the stare, and determined approach of Danny.

Shock and awe, Danny boy, shock and awe.

Accelerating, Danny hopped up the step into the bar. In one fluid movement he put all his body weight into a kick on the side of Aleksander knee. The result was brutal, it snapped the joint back the wrong way, dropping him screaming to the floor. At the same time, he powered the tyre wrench into the temple of the guy standing next to him. The blow sent him falling to the ground like a tree that had just been felled. Out of the corner of his eye he saw the guy at the bar reaching inside his jacket. Acting on impulse, Danny picked up the eight-ball and pitched it across the room. It struck the guy at the bar dead centre between the eyes, making a sound like a fast break as it fractured his skull. His head whipped back with the impact and he slid down the bar to a heap on the floor. Danny turned his attention to the last man standing on the other side of the pool table.

'I want no trouble,' he said in broken English, backing away slowly before turning and running out of the bar.

Danny checked out the barman. The old guy was still sitting behind the bar unimpressed with the whole scene. He raised his drink and shook his head, apparently not caring what they were doing. Aleksander cursed in pain as he rolled about on the floor. He reached for the gun in his jacket as he stared defiantly. Already ahead of him, Danny kicked him hard in the crotch, doubling him up in more pain. Danny reached down and relieved him of the gun and slid it into the back of his jeans. Coming back to Aleksander he dragged him across to the middle of the floor by the collar of his jacket and dumped him down.

'Where's the woman?' Danny said, standing over him.

'Fuck you, they will kill you for th—'

Danny cut him off short by pushing on his shattered knee with his foot. Aleksander screamed loudly, then gritted his teeth as he breathed heavily through the pain.

'Let's try that again. Where did you take the woman?'

When he didn't answer, Danny put more pressure on his knee.

'No, no. Fuck, stop, stop,' he shouted in pain.

'Where did they take her?'

'The... Fuck... The old coach depot in Valencia.'

'Where? The address,' Danny said, twisting his foot for additional pain.

'No, stop, stop. Valencia, Calle Riu Xaló. Valencia,' Aleksander replied through the gasps.

'What do they want with her?'

'They take her to Barcelona with the others, she's to be sold. You're dead. They'll fucking kill you for this.'

Unemotional and unimpressed, Danny raised his arm and cracked him in the face with the wrench, knocking him and several of his teeth out. Standing, he walked to the barman. Taking fifty euros out of his wallet, he slid it across the bar to the old guy.

'Call him an ambulance, ok?' said Danny to the nodding barman.

He was about to leave when he turned back

and slid another hundred across the bar and looked the barman in the eye.

'You didn't see a thing, ok?' he said keeping one finger on the money.

'I never do, señor,' he replied.

With that, Danny left the bar and made his way back to the car. He was looking up the address for the old coach depot when Scott's ringing interrupted his search.

'Daniel, where the hell are you, old man? I got back to the bar and the barman told me about a scuffle with some thugs over a woman. I swear I can't leave you alone for a minute,' said Scott, chuckling in his usual jovial manner.

'Sorry, Scott, I can't explain right now. I've got to go to Valencia, there's a woman in trouble. I'll call you later ok?'

Danny hung up without waiting for a reply, he had to get moving. Putting the address in the satnav on his phone, he started the engine and headed out of Altea.

THREE

The road to Valencia was good, it only took an hour and a half on the smooth dual carriageway. Danny found the old coach depot at the back of a large industrial estate on the edge of the city. It was old and neglected with a wall around it, but no gates. Parking around the corner, he walked beside the wall to the entrance. He took a peek, scanning the large tarmac parking area and the closed shutter doors. When he didn't see anyone he leaned in and checked the front of the building. Nothing. No cars, no people, all quiet.

Crossing to the corner of the building, he tucked in by the shutters and a metal door. He tried the handle and to his surprise found it unlocked. Danny slipped inside and found himself in an old locker room. Moving to the door, he opened it a crack and looked into the depot. The large space was empty apart from a white lorry parked in the centre with *Manos Distribución de Fruta* on the side with pictures of oranges and lemons. The black BMW from Altea sat parked beside it. What would have been the repair bay was only a short distance to one side of him. It still had the work benches and tool chests in place, although now they were mostly empty and rusting.

Danny scooted across to the benches and bobbed down as he moved along to the far corner. Looking through the gap between an oil drum and the bench, he got eyes on the lorry. A middle-aged man with a weathered face and pot belly appeared from behind the lorry. He shouted something in Albanian and a door opened on the far side to what must have been the depot offices. The driver from Altea with the scar stuck his head out and shouted something back. The guy from the lorry shook his head and walked over to him. They disappeared inside, leaving the depot quiet and empty.

A few minutes passed and nobody came back

out of the office door. Danny's plan to take a look in the offices changed when he heard thuds and muffled cries coming from the back of the lorry. Nobody came out of the door so he ran across the concrete to the back of the lorry. A padlock sat securely locked through the metal handle of its twin doors. Conscious of the time he was taking, Danny ran back to the repair bay and riffled through the drawers and cupboards. He found a large metal tyre lever tucked between some old engine parts. Grabbing it he ran back to the lorry, taking a little less care and stealth than he should have. Taking a quick look down the side of the lorry at the office door first, he shoved the iron through the padlock loop and cracked it downwards. His weight and the long leverage broke the lock open with a loud crack. Danny pulled the heavy door open. Huddled at the far end, twenty pairs of terrified eyes stared nervously back at him. The women were all young, late teens or early twenties, of various nationalities, probably tourists or migrants lured and kidnapped. Tucked in the middle was the woman from the car, her face turning from fear to recognition to hope.

'Come on, quick, quick,' Danny said, beckoning them over.

They didn't move straight away, fear and mistrust paralysing them to the spot. Only when the woman from the car took her first tentative steps towards him did the others dare to follow. The woman got within a few feet of him when the terror returned to her face. By the time Danny realised she was looking behind him, it was too late. He barely registered the blow to the back of his head before darkness swallowed him up.

Consciousness was slow to return. He kept his eyes shut and let his body tell him how he was doing.

Something wasn't right.

His arms were above his head and he was hanging off the ground. His hands were tied and hooked over something. With consciousness came pain. His head was splitting and he could feel the sticky trickle of blood running down the back of his neck. He opened his eyes, the fuzzy input of light hurting his head further.

'Hey, Lurik, pretty boy is awake,' shouted the chubby driver across the depot.

Danny looked up. His hands were tied and looped over a hook on an electric hoist suspending him two feet off the ground. He looked ahead of him just in time to see Lurik slam a fist into his ribs. Not having time to react and tense up, the blow knocked all the wind out of him leaving him coughing and struggling to breathe.

'Who are you, police, Interpol?' Lurik shouted into Danny's face.

'As soon as I get down from here I'm going to show you who I am,' Danny wheezed, his face hard and his eyes defiant.

Wham.

Lurik powered a blow to the ribs on the other side. Lurik turned away as Danny coughed his guts up.

'Valmir, we go. I want to be in Barcelona before five. You two stay here, beat him until he talks. Then kill him. You can join us later,' commanded Lurik throwing the keys for the BMW to two of his men. Joining the driver, Lurik climbed into the lorry cab before it thundered out of the depot in a cloud of diesel smoke.

FOUR

The two men watched the lorry go. One followed it to close the roller door—they would deal with Danny behind closed doors; the second moved towards Danny with a wicked grin on his face. Danny looked beaten and semi-conscious, but he'd been regaining his composure, breathing steadily, flexing his muscles, getting blood back into his hanging arms.

When the guy came in swinging his fists, Danny kicked him hard in the crotch. Winded and surprised the man doubled up. Immediately locking his thighs around the man's neck, Danny clamped down with all his might. He cut off the blood supply to the man's brain, rendering him unconscious inside of thirty seconds.

Across the depot, the sound of the roller doors coming down kept the first guy from hearing the scuffle behind him. Flexing his muscles, Danny swung his legs back and forth, lifting them more with every swing. When he'd gained enough momentum, he shot his legs upwards and pushed through with his arms and shoulders until he was upside down. Gripping the chain between his legs he lifted his tied wrists off the hook and grabbed it. Loosening his grip on the chain he rolled himself down and dropped, landing solidly on the concrete floor. He untied his hands and slowly raised his head, looking out from under his blood-caked unruly mop of hair. His face was as hard as granite and his eyes stared murderously at the lean Albanian just starting to turn his way.

Confusion, shock, and panic hit the man all at once. Suddenly he kicked himself into gear and made a break for the office door. Fuelled on adrenaline, fury and revenge, Danny hurtled across the depot after him, rugby tackling him before he reached the door. Flipping him over, Danny powered punches into his face, knocking away his feeble attempts to block them. His nose collapsed and his eyes started rolling back in his head. Just short of killing him, Danny got his rage in check and pulled back. When the man came round he was being dragged along by his feet, his arms trailing along the floor behind him. Danny dropped him in the middle of the repair bay and tied his feet together. Pressing the button to lower the hoist, Danny hooked his feet and raised him off the floor. He coughed blood as it ran down his broken nose to the back of his throat.

Danny sat in a chair looking at him, face to upside-down face.

'Where have they taken the women?' he said picking up a rag and dabbing the cut on the back of his head.

'Fuck you, you're a dead man,' the guy spat.

'Last chance. Where have they taken the women?'

The Albanian spouted a stream of obscenities in his native tongue.

Danny got up and walked past him. When he heard metallic clangs and squeaky wheels the Albanian swung about, craning his neck trying to see. Danny appeared in front of him with two big cylinders on a trolley. He unwound the oxyacetylene nozzle and turned the red and blue valves, sparking the lighter in front of it. There was a pop, and a jet of orange flame reflected in the Albanian's wide eyes. Playing with the valves, Danny turned the jet from orange to an intense blue.

'Right, first I'm going to burn your bollocks off, then your dick. If you still don't talk, I'm going to torch your eyeballs until they boil and pop,' Danny said, his face deadpan and his voice without humour.

He grabbed the guy's belt, holding him steady while he panicked and thrashed about. Moving the hissing blue flame closer, Danny held it close until the Albanian's trousers smouldered, giving off acrid black smoke.

'No, no, please stop. I'll tell you, please,' he shrieked.

Danny turned the valves off with a pop and threw the nozzle down. He grabbed the guy by the hair and pulled his head up to meet his face.

'Talk.'

'Club de striptease de Diamantes. Er, how

you say Diamonds Strip, they prepare the girls at Diamonds Strip Club before moving them to the auction house,' he said, talking quickly.

'Where? I need an address,' growled Danny.

'Carrer De Muntaner, Barcelona.'

The unconscious Albanian stirred behind him. Danny went over and searched him as he groaned. He found a Glock 17 tucked in a shoulder holster, took it and stood back.

'I told you what you want, let me go,' the hanging Albanian whimpered.

'Like you would have let me go, like you would have let the women go when they cried and pleaded?' Danny said with a growl.

'What? Fucking let me—'

Danny whipped the gun up, shooting him straight between the eyes.

The guy on the floor rolled on his back moaning. He opened his eyes at the sound of the gunshot. Danny walked past him putting two shots in the centre of his chest without even looking at him. Tucking the gun in the back of his jeans, he crossed to the BMW. He found the gun he'd taken off Aleksander on the passenger seat and tucked it next to the other one. He checked the car but found nothing other than a business card for Simon Mandes, Lawyer, at a Barcelona business address. Danny pocketed it and left the depot. Getting back to his car he looked at himself in the rear-view mirror. He was a mess. Standing outside he used the bottle of water he'd bought earlier to clean the dried blood off his neck and hands. He poured the rest of the bottle over his mop of hair, painfully rinsing the blood out. Looking a little less like a crazed killer, he set off for Barcelona.

FIVE

The white *Manos Distribución de Fruta* lorry beeped as it reversed into the alley down the side of Diamonds Strip Club. The gap was narrow and the doors tapped the brickwork as Lurik and Valmir got out. Lurik banged twice on the fire escape door at the rear of the club. Turning, he looked down the side of the lorry checking the coast was clear. The door opened behind him. A stern-faced middle-aged woman with brassy-yellow hair stood in the opening. She was short, slim and attractive in a hard sort of way. Standing behind her in stark contrast was a gorilla of a man, with clippered stubble for hair and a flat broken nose. He grinned at Lurik, exposing a row of gold front teeth.

'Elona, it is good to see you. Frenk, come, help me get the merchandise inside,' said Lurik as Valmir unlocked the door to the lorry. He pulled the doors back, causing the frightened women to cover their eyes from the sudden flood of daylight releasing them from their pitch-black journey.

'Come, move. All of you inside,' Lurik yelled at them.

They didn't move, no one wanting to go first. Like scared sheep staying in the flock. Lurik's anger grew. He banged the side of the lorry, shouting.

'I said move your arses, NOW! Frenk, get them out.'

Climbing in the back, the lorry rocked as Frenk stood up and moved to the rear. He grabbed the nearest woman and pushed her with ease towards the lorry doors. Moving round, he herded them out towards Lurik and Valmir who grabbed their arms and roughly pulled them down, moving them into the back of the club. When they were all inside, Lurik and the others pushed and bullied the cowering women up the stairs to a first-floor corridor with rooms along either side.

Elona moved amongst them, a friendly smile on her face. 'Come on, my dears. Elona will look after you. Just do as you are told and everything will be ok.'

Frenk and Valmir divided them up two to a room, pushing them in and pulling the door shut behind them. A large bolt secured each door, sliding into place with a soul-destroying metallic click.

Lurik appeared with a large bag he'd fetched from the lorry. He frowned when he heard the women pleading and crying from behind the locked doors.

'Hurry up and drug them. You have enough heroin, yes?'

'Yes, Lurik, Ervin is preparing it now,' said Elona, unimpressed by his mood.

'Good. I want them out of their clothes and looking good. Mandes has set everything up for this evening. I'll be in the office,' he said walking off without waiting for a reply.

'Ok let's get on with it, first one Frenk,' said Elona.

Frenk slid the bolt back and opened the door.

Elona stepped inside. The room was bare other than two single, metal-framed beds and a sink and toilet in the corner. There was no window, just a bare bulb hanging from the ceiling. Lingerie was spread neatly across the end of each bed next to a white silk dressing gown.

'Now, ladies, let's have no fuss. Take off your clothes and give them to me,' Elona said pleasantly.

'What the fuck? Let me out of here, you bitch,' shouted one of the women. She'd hardly got the words out of her mouth when Elona slapped the redhead around the face. The blow would sting like hell but wouldn't bruise; she didn't want to ruin the merchandise.

'Remove your clothes, my dears, you don't want to make things worse for yourselves.'

Shocked and crying they slowly undressed, trying to cover their nudity. Their vulnerability only went to enforce Elona's power over them.

'Now that wasn't hard, was it? Let's have a look at you.'

She inspected them and chose the underwear and stockings she wanted them to wear. The women looked at each other and reluctantly got dressed. The underwear was a horrifying hint to their future but was better than being naked.

'That's better. Don't worry, Ervin will be around shortly. He'll give you something to make it all feel better.'

Locking the door behind her, Elona made her way along the corridor repeating the performance and getting tough when needed. She'd just locked the last door when screaming came from the first room. She didn't hurry. Walking to the open door she glanced in. A woman was lying on the bed mumbling to herself, her eyes dilated and glazed. Ervin had his weight on top of the other woman, pinning her face down on the bed. He grabbed her arm as she struggled and bent it behind her, placing a tourniquet around the top. He waited for the veins to raise then, holding her still, he injected her with heroin. He only had to wait a few seconds before her eyes dilated and the fight left her. Enjoying his work, Ervin fondled her breast before getting up and walking out of the room, sliding the bolt into place behind him.

'Ervin, no funny business. Take the photos and send them to Mandes. I want top price for the girls, ok?' said Elona fixing him with a warning stare.

'Ok, ok,' he replied, picking two more needles off his tray.

Leaving him, she went upstairs to the office. Lurik was at the desk, a frown on his face. He sorted the women's belongings into piles of passports, driving licences, jewellery, and money. Looking at Elona he slid the passports and driving licences across the table.

'Tomorrow you take these to Stephan. Tell that slippery bastard not to fuck me about. Same price as last time, ok?'

'What is bothering you, Lurik,' she said walking around the desk and putting her arm around his shoulders.

'We had trouble in Altea, some Englishman.'

'What kind of trouble?'

'One of the girls got away, he tried to interfere. I warned him off then he turned up at the depot. Now I can't get hold of Aleksander, Ditmir or Pirro,' said Lurik looking at his mobile.

'Don't worry, my love. Aleksander is probably drunk again, and Ditmir and Pirro will be driving or out of signal. They will be here soon.'

'Yes, I suppose you're right. How are the women looking?'

'They are top quality, darling. We will make much   money   tonight.'

SIX

Navigating the busy city with one eye on the satnav and one eye on the road, Danny made his way to Carrer de Muntaner. He made a few wrong turns while Scott kept phoning him, knocking the satnav off the screen to display Scott's caller ID. Eventually Danny pulled over and answered.

'Scott, this really isn't the time, mate.'

'Pardon me for worrying, old boy. You disappear on some mercy mission then I don't hear from you for hours. I didn't know what to think,' said Scott slightly offended.

'Ok, ok, sorry. I'm in Barcelona. I've just got to check something out. If I'm right I'll call the authorities and let them deal with it,' Danny said, hoping the vague reasoning would be enough to satisfy Scott and get him off the phone.

'Ok, right. Well, call me when you're done and don't do anything stupid,' said Scott, his voice turning to concern.

'Ok, Dad, I'll call you later.'

'Mm, very funny. You can tell me all about it later.'

Satnav resumed, Danny continued his way through the tree-lined streets, taking in the mix of shops and apartment blocks rising from three to eight or ten storeys high. He turned into Carrer de Muntaner in the early evening as the sun turned orange and dropped in the sky.

Diamonds Strip Club took him a few minutes to find as he drove slowly along looking for a sign. Its façade was more subtle than he'd expected. The windows in the three-storey building had blacked-out glass with a black and silver sign, *Club de Caballeros de Diamantes*, above the closed entrance doors. Danny's limited Spanish was just about good enough to know it said 'gentlemen's club'. He drove past, noticing the alley to one side with the front of the white lorry tucked well back in the shadows. Finding a free parking bay fifty yards away, he pulled in and switched the engine off. He sat there for a few minutes turning the options over in his mind.

Call the police? Will they believe me? Possibly. Will they charge me with the assault on Aleksander and his mates in Altea and the murder of the two at the depot? Definitely.

Police ruled out, Danny made sure no one was looking and brought the Glock 17 out and checked it. Three rounds down, fourteen left in the magazine. Slipping it back into his jeans, he covered it with his top and got out of the car. Street lights started twinkling on, mirrored by shops and apartments down the road as the last of the sun's rays fell below the horizon. A large diesel engine echoed from the alley next to Diamonds as the lorry started up.

Danny rolled behind one of the trees on his side of the road, keeping in the shadows as the lorry's headlights cut past the tree and illuminated the shopfront either side of him. The engine revved and the lorry pulled out onto the street, driving away like any other unremarkable delivery lorry.

The lights masked the lorry's cab. Danny could only make out the silhouettes of two people in the cab, their outlines too dark to tell who they were. Stepping out from cover Danny turned his attention back to the club. It was still early and the club wasn't open yet. The front doors were heavy and firmly shut. Moving to the side he looked down the empty alley. With the lorry gone it was dark and shadowy. The only light came from a dim bulkhead lamp above the fire escape door at the rear of the building. Spotting a camera looking down the alley from the front of the club and one above the fire escape door at the rear, Danny stayed outside the alley. Backing away he looked up and down the road. Seeing what he wanted Danny headed off, stopping outside a sportswear shop further down the road. He was looking for something in the overflowing bins in an alcove, but seeing his reflection in the shop window he went in. A few minutes later he came out with a navy blue fleece jacket and a black baseball cap. Putting them on, he rooted around the side of the big bin and fished out a couple of medium-sized

boxes.
  Perfect.

SEVEN

With his cap pulled low, Danny walked casually down the alley, boxes in hand. In the gloom he looked just like any other delivery man. He banged the door twice loudly and waited.

'Quién es?' came a shout from inside asking who it was.

'Entrega,' Danny shouted back, hoping the Spanish the sports shop attendant had told him was actually Spanish for delivery.

'Ok, ok,' came a shout and a clunk as a bolt was unlocked.

The door swung open and Ervin stood facing him. Danny handed the boxes forward and Ervin instinctively took them off him. He frowned, looking down in momentary confusion at the lightness of the empty boxes. When he looked up all he saw was Danny's fist a split-second before it hit him full on between the eyes. Ervin flew back inside, dropping the boxes as he slid down the wall behind him. Bending over him Danny powered a few more punches in for good measure. He gave Ervin a couple of kicks satisfied he was out for the count he turned and closed the fire escape door behind him.

He was in a small square room off a main corridor. To the left lay stairs to the rear of the building, to the right was the bar and drinks cellar on. Chucking Ervin over his shoulder, Danny pushed the drinks cellar door open and carried him in. After tucking him out of sight behind a wall of beer crates, Danny took a gun out and made his way to the stairs. Moving cautiously, he opened the door on the first-floor landing, just far enough to see through. With no sound and nobody in sight he slid inside. A corridor with door either side stretched ahead of him.

Gripping the bolt on the first door, he slid it back and pushed it slowly open. The room was empty. Danny had a bad feeling in the pit of his stomach. Moving fast, he checked the other rooms.

Empty.

Shit, they must have been in the lorry.

Anger growing inside him, he took some deep breaths and went back to the stairs, moving quietly to the next floor. There were changing rooms and toilets off the landing to the right; a room with La Oficina written on it lay on the left. Danny took it to mean office. He put his ear to the door and listened. It was quiet, no talking, but he was sure he could hear someone moving about. With his gun at the ready he pushed the door open. Sweeping his gun across the room he levelled on a target. Elona stood by the window. She jumped, looking terrified at his arrival.

'Please, please don't hurt me. I know I'm not supposed to be in here. I'm sorry,' she cried shaking.

'Shh, it's ok. I'm not going to hurt you. I just want to know where they took the women from the lorry?' said Danny, tucking his gun back in his jeans.

'I don't know about any women. They force me to work in the club and keep the customers happy.'

'It's ok. I'll get you out of here in a minute,' Danny said, spotting passports and ID by some money and jewellery on the desk.

He went around the desk and checked the papers and drawers. The only thing that stood out was the lawyer Simon Mandes's name on a post-it note with an address and 8 p.m. written on it. Tearing it off, Danny put it in his pocket and picked up Lurik's bag. Sliding all the women's stuff inside it, he hooked it over his shoulder.

'Come on, I'll take you somewhere safe,' said Danny, reaching his hand out to Elona.

She took it and moved close. When Danny took the lead to leave, she stooped, sliding a razor-sharp knife out of her boot. Feeling her body shift, Danny turned back in time to see a knife heading for his neck. He jerked back. The knife missed its target and buried itself into his shoulder. She pulled it out a split-second later and came at him again, screaming like a banshee.

Elona caught him across the chest as he moved out of her way; the knife only cut his clothes. As the blade came in again, his muscle memory fell back on combat training. He caught her wrist and forced the knife inwards and upwards, plunging the blade up into her chest between the ribs to pierce her heart. She swore at him in Albanian before coughing up blood, convulsing and losing consciousness.

His shoulder hurt like hell but it still moved relatively ok. Picking himself up, he pulled one of the guns and went to leave. Reaching for the office door, it flew inwards catching him by surprise. Before he knew it, Frenk's powerhouse frame charged him. Grabbing his gun barrel he twisted it out of his hand. Lifting Danny up with ease, Frenk threw him across the office, sending him bouncing off the top of the desk and onto the floor in a flutter of papers and shower of pens and utensils. Grunting, Danny reached behind him to get the other gun. When he touched bare back, his eyes darted around the mess trying to find it. On the other side of the desk Frenk saw Elona's body on the floor and exploded with rage. He roared and grabbed the desk, flipped it into the corner of the room exposing Danny on the floor behind it.

Oh shit.

Shovel-like hands gripped Danny around the throat, lifting him off the ground. Scrabbling around the floor before his feet left the ground, Danny grabbed a stapler by his side. Fighting the immense pressure on his neck, Danny flipped the stapler open and rapidly punched at the side of Frenk's face. After half a dozen hits, Danny still had no reaction. Fighting the dizziness building in his head, he punched a staple into the centre of Frenk's eyeball. Screaming, Frenk released his grip and staggered back, his hands covering his face.

Danny coughed and wheezed as he sucked in deep breaths. Ducking down, he threw papers out the way hunting for his gun. He spotted it in the corner and dived in its direction. At the same time, a mad, crazed Frenk charged after him. He grabbed Danny's ankle just as he got his fingers on the grip of the gun, and dragged Danny back into the room. Turning himself over, Danny levelled the gun and put two in the chest and one in the forehead. Frenk dropped to his knees, his brain dead while his body played catch-up. The staple glinted across the pupil of his eye as he fell flat on his face.

'Thank fuck for that,' said Danny out loud.

Searching the debris on the floor, Danny found the other gun and the bag of the women's belongings. He straightened himself up and took the lawyer's address out of his pocket. Putting it into the satnav, he walked out of the office.

EIGHT

Towards the back of Barcelona, where the houses got bigger and the swimming pools got larger, they worked their way into the hills. Valmir backed the lorry down the side of a large enclosed mansion. The back door opened and an immaculately-dressed Spaniard with wavy, slicked-back hair and olive skin stepped out. He smiled at Lurik with a perfect row of white teeth.

'Good evening, Lurik,' he said, friendly and polite.

'Simon,' Lurik said curtly.

'Why the long face, my friend? Is there something wrong with the merchandise?'

'No, no. Everything is good. It's been a long day,' replied Lurik, throwing the lorry doors open.

Simon's eyes lit up at the sight of the drugged and confused women all clad in lingerie and silk dressing gowns. They sat or lay on blankets, some quiet, some trying to say something or protest, their minds too clouded to make themselves heard.

'Lovely ladies, let's get you inside,' said Simon, standing to one side as Valmir helped them down one by one.

Some of Simon's men came out as they steadied the women who were wobbling in high heels on uneasy legs.

'You haven't given them too much?' said Simon, his tone turning cold.

'No, by the time of the auction they will be steadier but still complacent.'

'Good, excellent,' said Simon, changing back to friendly and polite.

Lurik followed Simon inside. His men took the women down a staircase to a room in the cellar. Simon took Valmir into the banqueting room; a huge table ran for most of its length. Places were set like a conference room, with a telephone, bound folder and numbered paddle neatly positioned in each place setting. At the far end they pushed two large wooden boxes together to form a makeshift stage. Large TV screens sat on trolleys either side of the boxes. They displayed a feed from a high-definition camera set up on a tripod in front of the stage.

'Is it all ready?' asked Lurik looking unimpressed as he always did. Money talked, everything else was just something you had to do to get it.

'Relax, the brokers will arrive soon. The video feed goes live at eight and the bids will start via phone link. We record the auction to promote the next event,' said Simon as he walked around the table revelling in his cleverness. He'd used his contacts as a top criminal lawyer to tap into and grow a client list with very specific tastes and appropriate funds to satisfy them.

'Good, you take care of this. I will take care of the women,' said Lurik. Leaving Simon he took the stairs down to the holding room in the cellar.

NINE

Driving through the millionaires' houses, Danny climbed through the hills on the outskirts of the city. He found the address, or rather he found the number on the high wall by the entrance to the property. Driving past he noticed two security men either side of the entrance. He turned down the side of the property and parked up close to the wall. Danny untied the fleece he'd secured tightly around his shoulder. It had stemmed the bleeding for now and the drying blood was holding the knife wound together. He checked the guns; eleven bullets in one and a full mag in the other.

Danny psyched himself up, controlling his anger and aggression for the task ahead. He got out and hopped up onto the rental car's roof. Jumping up, he pulled himself painfully onto the top of the wall. There were a good deal of plants, trees and foliage concealing him from the house and gate. Jumping down into the bushes, he watched as cars started arriving. Weaving his way along the wall, Danny moved under cover towards the mansion. He squatted behind a wood store to one side and continued to watch as suited men stepped up to the door. Two more security men greeted them at the door where they handed over an invitation before being shown inside. As more cars arrived, their parking got progressively closer to Danny's hiding place.

When the final car drove up, it parked only a few metres away from him. A big guy got out, around Danny's size, chubbier, with the look of a pen-pusher. Seizing the chance, Danny rushed out and threw an arm around his neck while clamping a hand over his mouth. He dragged him behind the wood store without much of a fight. The guy wasn't strong or fit; he floundered around with a panicked look on his face, trying to get a breath. Danny tightened his grip like a vice, squeezing ever tighter. As soon as he'd passed out, Danny stripped him and changed, and emerged a minute later suited-up with an invitation in his hand. Moving with an air of arrogance Danny walked up the steps. Simon's security greeted him. Keeping his cool, Danny flicked the invite at them and moved into the hallway without paying them any attention. A second of nerves followed by a mass of option and action calculations went through his head as the immaculately groomed Simon Mandes stood in his way.

'Good evening. Please hurry. You're the last. Come, we are about to go live. You are Mr Zimmerman's broker, yes?'

'Er, yes, that's correct,' said Danny, relieved his cover wasn't blown.

Simon ushered him into the banqueting hall and showed him to his place around the huge table. Danny glanced around at the eight other brokers, pleased that none of them wished to engage in conversation. They were here for business and business only.

Soft-talking murmurs echoed round the room as the brokers sat on the phones to their buyers.

They flicked through the folders, talking and making notes while nervously toying with their numbered paddles, eager to start. Danny opened the folder and flicked through the pages of what looked like a catalogue of women. He picked up the phone and put it to his ear to fit in with the others. Turning the page, he saw the picture and description of the woman from Altea. She was dressed in lingerie her face expressionless and her eyes distant and unfocused, lost in a drug haze. As Danny lingered on the page, a voice on the other end of the phone surprised him.

'Hanz, where the hell have you been? You nearly missed the start,' shouted Zimmerman down the phone.

Danny was about to answer while thumbing through more pages of women in the folder, when Simon opened proceedings from a podium at the front.

'Gentlemen, we are now live,' he said tapping his laptop. The screens either side of the stage burst into life as the feed was broadcast via the dark web to the buyers around the world.

'Good evening. You are all aware of the rules.

The auctioneer's word is final. There will be no refunds or exchanges. The winning bids must be paid and verified prior to the shipping of goods. If there are no questions, let us begin,' said Simon, waiting a couple of seconds in case anyone spoke. With all eyes on him to start, he waved to one of his men on the door to the left of the stage. Danny noticed it was the same man who'd been at the front door to greet him. Still working through scenarios in his head, Danny watched the girl from page one being led in by the second man from the front door.

Two on the gate, two inside, plus Lurik and the lorry driver—Valmir, and Simon Mandes—but he doesn't look like a fighter. Six to deal with and the element of surprise.

I've had worse odds.

The guard led the woman by the arm as she walked unsteadily towards the stage. He put her in the centre and took the silk dressing gown off her. She stood swaying on high heels, her wide eyes drawn to the crystal chandelier hanging from the ceiling. She was mesmerised by its twinkling lights and oblivious to the skimpy lingerie she was wearing.

'Shall we start the bidding at ten thousand?' said Simon, watching the room. Number two's paddle went up followed by number six's.

'Ten, that's twenty. Any adv—Thirty bid. I have thirty thousand from number three.'

'Forty thousand,' came an excited voice down Danny's phone.

Not wanting to give the game away he raised his paddle.

'Forty from number nine. Any advance on forty? A half. Yes, forty-five thousand back to number three. Any more bids? Going once, going twice. Sold to number three,' said Simon banging his gavel on the podium.

The guard pulled the woman off the stage and guided her out the door. He appeared moments later with the woman from Altea. They put her onstage and left her standing like the first woman, not completely out of it but drugged enough not to comprehend what was going on or where her fate may take her.

The bidding was just about to start when the doors to the banqueting hall burst open and the two armed security guards from the gate appeared with a distressed Hanz standing in between them, embarrassed in his underwear.

TEN

'What is the meaning of this?' yelled Simon, furious at the intrusion.

'Sir, someone jumped Mr Zimmerman's broker by his car and—'

'That's him, he's the one who attacked me!' shouted Hanz, his face turning red as he pointed.

Danny turned sideways in his chair, one hand tucked inside his suit jacket. He looked at Hanz like he was mad. 'Don't be ridiculous.'

Using the moment of confusion, Danny opened fire on the guards. Aiming wasn't possible with his right hand pointing backwards around his left side. Tufts of suit material flew through the air as Danny shot from inside his jacket, going for as close to centre mass as possible. He caught one guard in the shoulder and throat before he got his gun out. Looking at his colleague choking on the floor, the other guard dived out of the room for cover. Danny managed to get him in the kneecap as he disappeared out of sight, screaming in agony.

The room erupted into panic as the brokers dived under the table or ran for their lives. Mandes's security guards on the other side of the room opened fire on Danny. The solid mahogany table was thick enough to hold the bullets off as he ducked behind it. Stuck there under cover, Danny got showered with bits of plastic phone, splinters, and splatters of blood as brokers got hit in the crossfire. Looking under the table, he fast-crawled past its tree-trunk-sized legs, sliding out the other side with a gun in each hand. He opened fire, catching the gunmen by surprise. There was no missing his target this time; peppered with bullets, they dropped like a stone. Danny's aim changed, focusing on Simon. He was holding the woman from Altea around the throat, using her as a shield in front of him. He had a small Ruger LC9s handgun to her head and was nervously bobbing in and out of sight behind her.

'Let her go, Mandes,' Danny said in a clear, commanding voice.

'Who are you? What do you want, money? I have money. We can come to some kind of arrangement,' said Simon, trying to make a deal the only way he knew how—with money.

'Let her go,' repeated Danny slightly louder, staring along the sights of his gun as he held it rock-steady in his hand.

Simon's head poked out of cover to negotiate some more. There was no deal: Danny took the shot. Simon's head whipped back as the bullet caught him between the eyes. A plume of red mist, bone and brains filled the air behind him as the bullet exited the back of his head. The woman stood in shock on the stage, the noise and blood and bullets cutting through her drug haze as her body's own adrenaline sobered her up. She looked at Danny in a moment of clarity. 'It's you, you came for me,' she said, tears trickling from her eyes.

'You and the others. Where are they?' Danny said with a reassuring smile.

'I don't know, my head was so fuzzy...
Downstairs, a basement I think. Through there.'
She pointed through the side door.

Danny picked up the silk dressing gown and
put it around her. Taking her hand, he led her
out of the room into the hallway. Stairs went
down on one side; the door to the side of the
house and the lorry on the other. Danny opened
the side door and went to the lorry cab. It was
empty, and the keys were still in it.

'What's your name?' he said.

'Maria.'

'Ok, Maria, I want you to get in the cab and
lock the door. I'm going to get the others then
I'll be straight back,' he said looking her straight
in the eyes to make sure she understood.

She looked scared but nodded and climbed up
into the cab.

'I'll be right back,' he said with a smile.

She locked the door and managed a smile
back. Danny turned and walked back into the
house. His face changed: hardened, angry and
determined. He checked the guns. Discovering
one was empty, he threw it on the ground and
headed down the stairs.

ELEVEN

The bottom of the stairs opened out into a large room with three passageways leading away through the foundations of the house. It was fairly well lit with whitewashed walls reflecting the strip lights above. Danny stood listening. He could hear murmurs, but the sound echoed off the walls and concrete floor making it difficult to determine direction. Taking the first passage, he edged slowly along until it opened out into a large wine cellar. Valmir sat in a chair helping himself to an expensive red. His gun sat on the chair next to him. He froze mid-glug, the bottle in the air, eyes locked on Danny.

Don't do it, you ain't gonna win.

Valmir stupidly went for the gun. He had no

chance of getting to it. Danny put two in his chest. Valmir looked down in disbelief before dropping the bottle and slumping in the chair.

Without delay Danny moved back along the passage to the first room. It was a toss-up between the other two passages, so Danny just took the next one along. He could see it open up ahead and could hear voices or sobbing. It was hard to tell over a growing motor noise, but it was definitely female. He came into a dimly-lit plant room with two huge boilers that heated the mansion. Their pipes split and snaked around before going up and across the ceiling. It was hot and loud from the pumps and boiler burners. On the far side he could see a heavy door secured in place by a large sliding bolt. He could hear the women on the other side and moved towards it.

Lurik spun out from the shadows behind a boiler, swinging a shovel with all his might. It caught Danny in the chest, knocking the wind out of him and the gun out of his hand. Landing flat on his back, he looked up just in time to see Lurik with both hands raised on the handle of the shovel, preparing to bring it down like a guillotine. Danny rolled to one side as the blade clanged on concrete, sparking as it chipped fragments off the floor. Kicking out from the ground, Danny swiped the back of Lurik's knees. His legs buckled as he went down on his back, swinging the shovel as he went. Danny caught the handle and pushed it towards the red-hot water pipe beside them, sandwiching Lurik's knuckles between the shovel handle and the metal surface. He screamed as the skin blistered and peeled, the pain and adrenaline giving him new-found strength. He kicked out hard, pushing Danny back as he let go of the shovel. Danny followed Lurik's eyes as they darted about looking for his dropped gun. Spotting it laying equal distance between them Lurik lunged to retrieve it. Danny made no attempt to beat him, he just stayed where he was, shovel in hand. Lurik Stood with his arm extended and gun levelled at Danny's head a wicked smile spreading across his face.

'I should have killed you in Altea.'

'Yes, you should,' replied Danny, his voice calm, his eyes dark and dangerous.

Lurik pulled the trigger, a look of confusion

taking a second or so to appear as the empty gun went *click* and Danny remained standing.

Before Lurik had time to react, Danny swung the shovel with two hands, gripping its handle like a baseball bat. The blade sliced through the air horizontally. It made contact with Lurik's throat, ripping it open. Arterial spray hit the hot pipes and steamed on contact. Lurik fell to his knees, clutching the wound as if he could somehow put it back together. Eventually his eyes rolled back in his head and he fell face down on the concrete. Dragging him out of the walkway, Danny took off his suit jacket and laid it over the bulk of the blood. He made his way to the locked door, slid the bolt back, and opened it. The women huddled in the corner, the heroin wearing off and fear returning.

'It's ok, I'm here to help. You're all going home.'

He held out his hand to the nearest. She shook nervously as he smiled to reassure her. Slowly she reached out and took his hand. The others followed her, kicking off their high heels to pad along in stockinged feet. Danny grabbed a couple of torches from a shelf and led the women out of the cellar, up the stairs and out to the lorry. He tapped on the door, pleased to see Maria's face appear at the window. She got out and joined the others.

'Here, take the torches and get in the lorry. I'm going to take you to people who will help you. They will look after you and get you back to your families, ok?'

Hope returning, the women nodded. Danny opened the lorry door and helped them up. Maria was last to go. He stopped before helping her up.

'Maria, I need you all to do something for me,' he said, looking her in the eye.

Her dark brown eyes looked up at him. She nodded before she spoke.

'What do you need us to do?'

TWELVE

Inside Barcelona's large concrete and glass police headquarters, officers and desk staff went about their business. The normality of the evening changed when an almighty bang and a crunching sound came from outside. A cacophony of car alarms followed, wailing their protest. Following a well-rehearsed procedure, the alarm was hit and police officers in full riot gear spilled out of the building expecting a possible terrorist attack.

What greeted them was a large white lorry with *Manos Distribución de Fruta* on the side. It was half on the pavement and half in the road. The front was bent and scratched where it had written-off parked police cars that were now sitting crushed on either side. The driver's door was open and the cab empty. When the officers entered the cab, they found a bag full of passports, ID, driving licences, and the camera from the auction. Cries and shouts from the back interrupted them, and officers surrounded the lorry's loading doors. Two officers pulled them open while armed guards pointed rifles towards the interior. Twenty pairs of eyes stared back at them from where they sat huddled around   two   torches.

THIRTEEN

Walking down the stairs of the little boutique hotel in Altea, Danny wandered out into the bright Mediterranean sunshine. He joined Scott on the restaurant terrace. He sat down slowly, his white cotton shirt hiding a multitude of cuts, scrapes and bruises, not to mention a stab wound to the shoulder.

'Rough night, old boy?' Scott said, chuckling at the state of him.

'You could say that,' replied Danny ordering coffee and croissants from the waiter.

'Did the damsel in distress show her appreciation for being rescued?' said Scott, raising his eyebrows and grinning like a schoolboy.

Danny managed a laugh, even though it hurt his ribs to do so.

'How did the house hunting go?' he said, changing the subject.

'Mm, I'm not sure about the location. I may come back and look somewhere a little livelier, like Barcelona.'

'Well, it's definitely livelier, mate,' said Danny, chuckling at his private joke.

'Talking of Barcelona, did you see the news? Someone drove a lorry full of scantily clad young ladies into the police headquarters. It turns out someone saved them from a human trafficking crime syndicate who sold them at some sort of perverted sex slave auction. Terrible affair.'

'Did they say who saved them?' Danny asked, his interest piqued.

'According to the women it was two Spanish guys with masks and guns. They burst into the auction at some high-profile lawyer's house and shot a whole lot of bad guys before driving the women to the police station. They crashed the van into the police cars parked out front and legged it. Quite bizarre, I must say,' said Scott, shaking his head.

'Very strange, mate. Anyway, what time is our flight, Scotty boy?' said Danny, thankful the women had told the police what he wanted them to.

'Twelve thirty, which means we better get the hire car back. Speaking of hire cars, is there any good reason why there's dirty great footprints on the roof of it?'

'Really, Scott? That's odd,' Danny said with a shrug.

The Timekeepers Box

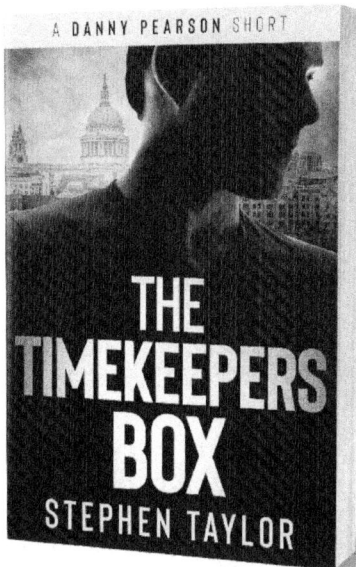

ONE

'Right, I'm off now, Rob,' said Danny rinsing out the last of the paintbrushes in the kitchen sink.

'Ok, cheers for the help, bruv,' came a shout from upstairs.

He dried his hands and slipped his jacket on. As he headed for the front door, he poked his head into the lounge. 'See you later, Tina. Take care of my niece or nephew, ok?' he said grinning at his sister-in-law.

'Ok, Danny, thanks for helping with the baby's room. You know what Rob's like, he gets more paint on himself than the walls,' she replied trying to get out of the sofa with the weight of her pregnant belly slowing her down.

'Don't get up on my account. I can see myself out,' Danny said, waving her back down.

'It's alright, I've gotta get up and stretch my legs. I think this one's learning to tap dance today,' she said, patting her belly.

She gave him a kiss on the cheek as she passed, shouting, 'See ya,' as she waddled into the kitchen.

Danny left Rob's house—the same house that used to be their parents, and the same one they'd both grown up in. Now it would be the same house the next generation would grow up in. Danny loved that house. He headed off home, which was a two-mile wander through the London suburb of Walthamstow. The summer evening air was still warm with the heat of the day, and the high street was still busy with people going this way and that. He looked over at Pullman's Gym with a guilty feeling, making a mental note to get back into training in the morning. He turned off the high street towards his house. His mobile rang as he slid the key in his front door. Pulling the phone out of his pocket, he smiled at the caller ID.

'Chaz, mate, it's been a while. What can—'

said Danny, silenced by Chaz's panicked voice as he closed the door behind him.

'No time, mate. I've just had a bunch of Syrian fuckers beating on my arse. They kept going on about some fucking box; said we took it from their mosque in Zaidal back when we were in the Regiment. I don't know what the fuck they're on about, but they mean business. I had to dive through the kitchen window to get away from them. Look, I'm on my way to yours. Warn Fergus and Smudge, and Danny, watch your back,' shouted Chaz over a car's engine noise.

'Roger that, I'll call them now. See you soon, mate.'

Danny hit the call button for Fergus the second Chaz rang off.

'Hi, this is Fergus McKinsey. I can't come to the phone right now. Leave a message and I'll get back to you.'

'Fergus, this is Danny Pearson. We've got a code red. Call me ASAP, and Fergus, watch your back, brother,' said Danny, keeping it short. He hit the call button for Smudge a second later.

'This number is no longer in use,' came back down the phone at him.

'Shit,' he said. The hairs on the back of his neck stood on edge as the feeling that something in the house wasn't right creeped across him.

Reaching for the umbrella stand in the hall, he slid an old baseball bat out, taking care not to tap it on the sides. Moving silently, he ducked his head into the lounge to see four serious-looking Syrians turning it upside down. The scene froze as all eyes locked on Danny. Seeing one guy pull a gun, Danny ducked back out and flew down the hall, sliding sideways into the kitchen. He was going for the back door but came face-to-face with three more Syrians instead. Using their surprise to his advantage, Danny kicked the small kitchen table into two of them while powering the baseball bat into the side of the third's head. It made a similar sound to a batter hitting a home run as the young man hit the deck hard. While the other two struggled to get past the table, someone from the lounge grabbed Danny's bat as he swung it back to attack them. Another man threw his arm around Danny's neck to drag him back. Letting go of the bat, Danny threw him forward over his shoulder. As the guy crashed to the ground, Danny immediately rammed his elbow back into the face of the man holding his bat behind him. The impact shattered bone and cartilage and he went down with blood pouring from his nose.

Danny was in full attack mode now, his face set in stone as his eyes darted around, targeting his next move. As the two in front flipped the kitchen table out of the way, Danny powered forward, kicking one in the balls so hard his feet left the ground, while cracking the other with a full-force left hook.

'Enough!' yelled someone from behind him.

The shout froze the room. Danny turned to see a lean middle-aged man with another man beside him. One pointed a Glock at his head, the other a Beretta. Danny stood breathing heavily and shaking slightly from the adrenaline still pumping round his body.

'Go on then, fucking do it,' he said, staring defiantly at them.

'Now, now, Mr Pearson. My name is Hasan Kassab and you have something that belongs to my family.'

'What makes you think that?' Danny said, playing for time as his mind ran through all possible escape scenarios.

'Let's not waste time, my friend. Three years ago your government destroyed half of our village, Zaidal, in Syria. The airstrike and your raid to find the Isis commander, Mahdi Al-Sarat, was undertaken on false information leaked by the very people you were trying to capture. During your mission, one of you was seen entering the ruins of our most sacred mosque and taking an ancient box from us. This wasn't just any box; it was a very rare and holy artefact given to my family in the 15th century by Mohammad Al-Hamawi, the timekeeper at the Umayyad Mosque in Damascus. Inside the box were the rosary beads of the great 9th century prophet, Elijah. It has taken three long years and the will of Allah to find you and your team. You will return our property to us or we will kill your friend Fergus McKinsey.'

'How do I know you've got him?' said Danny studying Hasan's calm face, his immaculately groomed beard and coarse black hair. His eyes showed no fear as he handed Danny a phone.

'Fergus?' Danny said.

'Danny? Tell these bastards to go fuck themselves.'

'You alright?'

'Yeah, the tossers jumped me. I'm chained up in some contain—'

The line went dead.

'You lay a finger on him and I'll kill the fucking lot of ya,' Danny said, his eyes blazing with an inner fury.

'We are men of faith, Mr Pearson. My brothers and I have no fear of death. Allah will protect us; who will protect you?' said Hasan. He nodded to his men who coughed, wheezed and limped their way past him towards the front door. When only Hasan remained, he tucked his gun inside his jacket and calmly turned and walked away.

'The clock's ticking, Mr Pearson. Return our property to us and I will release Mr McKinsey unharmed.'

TWO

Danny uprighted the kitchen table and picked up the baseball bat. He wandered along the hall, pushing the front door shut before glancing at the mess in the living room.

Shit. Better check upstairs.

He went up to find they'd turned over all the rooms in their search for the box. After straightening and tidying up the worst of it, Danny left the rest, picked the bat up and went back downstairs. He'd just turned from the bottom step when the front door burst open. Danny had the bat up and ready to strike in a split second.

'Whoa, shit, no! It's Chaz!'

Recognition kicked in just before Danny took

his head off.

'Nice to see you, Charlie boy,' said Danny dumping the bat back in the umbrella stand and giving his old SAS buddy a customary hug and slap on the back.

'Did you get hold of Fergus and Smudge?' said Chaz noticing the carnage in the living room.

'The Syrians have got Fergus, and Smudge's phone's disconnected,' said Danny turning his back on Chaz and walking to the kitchen.

'Fuck, they were here? What happened?'

'Come through, I'll tell you all about it.'

Danny picked the kitchen chairs up and found the kettle in the mess. After dumping mugs of hot tea on the table, he sat down next to Chaz.

'Go on then, what happened after I called?' said Chaz.

'Do you remember the Syrian mission to take out Isis leader Mahdi Al-Sarat?'

'Yeah, little town, Zaidal. We went in after an airstrike to find him, but it was bad intel, Al-Sarat was never there,' said Chaz running it through his head.

'When I got off the phone with you, the house was full of Syrians—lean, tough little fuckers. I was working my way through them when their leader, Hasan Kassab, stuck a gun to my head. He passed me a phone with Fergus on the other end. He's ok, they've got him tied up in a container somewhere. Apparently, they saw one of us take their mega-religious box containing rosary beads from some 9th century prophet, Elijah or something. The whole village worships the bloody thing and they've been searching for the men who took it for the last three years. We give them the fucking box back or they kill Fergus.'

'I don't know anything about a box, do you?' said Chaz thinking out loud.

The two men looked at each other in a lightbulb moment before speaking in unison.

'Smudge.'

'Got to be. I was always having a go at him about taking souvenirs,' said Danny, rummaging through the turfed-up kitchen drawer behind him. He eventually found a tatty old address book and started flicking through the pages.

'What you looking for?' said Chaz.

'Smudge has a sister, Kelly. I helped Smudge move her into a flat a few years ago, somewhere in Wandsworth. I've got her address somewhere in here… Yep, here it is,' said Danny, turning the book around to show Chaz.

'Great fucking reunion this is, we must do it more often,' chuckled Chaz.

'Come on, let's go and find that dipshit Smudge, and hope he's got a little fucking box on him,' said Danny, managing a grin as he got up.

'My car's outside, we can go in that.'

'What you got?'

'I borrowed the wife's Nissan Micra. Luckily, she's at her sister's for a few days cos she's going to go nuts when she comes home and finds the house all busted up,' said Chaz following Danny to the door.

'I think we'll take my car.'

'Whatever, mate, I don't m— whoa, ok, we're taking your car,' said Chaz as the locks on Danny's BMW M4 popped open with a touch of the keyring.

They slid into the leather sports seats. Danny put the address in the sat nav for Smudge's sister, Kelly. He fired up the car with a deep throaty rumble before gunning it down the road.

THREE

As it happened, they would have got to Wandsworth just as quick in the Micra. London's early evening traffic was bumper-to-bumper. It took them over an hour to crawl across the capital into south London and the suburbs of Wandsworth. The sat nav directed them to two council tower blocks that had seen better days. Parking on the road outside the estate, Danny and Chaz headed across the recreation ground by a five-a-side football pitch towards the entrance doors. The sun dipped below the horizon beyond the tower blocks, leaving the entrance doors shrouded in orange-lit shadows. Like a pack of hyenas, a group of young men slipped out of the passageways.

There were about ten of them, all different sizes, all swaggers and false bravado, with eyes hidden under pulled-up hoodies. Their formation tightened up in front of Danny and Chaz, blocking their way to the doors.

'I fink you must be lost, bruv,' said one of the larger guys stepping to the front of the gang. Tilting his head back to expose a pasty face and bad teeth, he puffed out his chest to look bigger.

'Oh, I don't think I am. Bruv,' said Danny, his body language changing, instantly tensing and flexing, ready for action.

'You gotta pay to cross our estate. What you got then, big man?' said a shorter black guy stepping to the front next to his gang leader. He reached inside his jacket and pulled out a hunting knife, pointing it at them as he glared with hate in his eyes.

'What you going to do with that, make me a sandwich?' said Chaz smirking.

The comment and Danny and Chaz's apparent lack of intimidation by the gang made them angry and nervous at the same time. They tightened ranks and moved forward a little.

'Look, grandad, we ain't fucking about here.

Give us your wallets and phones. Now,' said the guy with the knife, stepping forward.

Chaz was waiting for the move. As soon as the youth was inside striking range, he shot a hand out and grabbed the back of his knife hand. Flicking the black guy's wrist in and up with lightning speed and power, it made a loud snapping sound which was followed by its owner screaming in pain. The knife rattled onto the concrete.

The tall pasty guy was shocked into action. He reached behind him and pulled a gun out of the back of his jeans. Danny had already seen it coming, playing out in slow-motion in his head. He lunged in, pushing the gun arm up with one hand while landing a punch to the throat with the other. The gun went off as Pasty Face went down, causing the gang to freak out and scatter in different directions.

'Nice move, Chaz,' said Danny grinning as he picked the gun up from beside the choking youth. He flicked the bullet out of the chamber and slid the magazine out of the grip. Looking around, he walked over and dropped them down a nearby drain. Effortlessly stripping the gun, Danny threw the slide into a bottle bank and the grip into a clothes bin by the tower block doors.

'Mm thanks, I'm a bit rusty. Yours was good though. I liked the throat punch, very effective,' Chaz said grinning. He picked up the knife and shoved it into the drain grill. With a hearty wrench, he snapped the blade off, hearing it plop into the water deep below. Stepping over the black guy as he rolled around clutching his broken wrist, Chaz put the handle into the bottle bank. Ignoring the two on the ground, Danny and Chaz pressed the buzzer for Smudge's sister.

'Hello,' came a nervous reply.

'Hi, Kelly, it's Danny Pearson, a friend of Smudge's. I helped Smudge to move you in. I'm trying to find him.'

'Oh yeah, hi, Danny. Come up. Did you hear a gunshot?' she said as the lock buzzed open.

'Nah, I think it was a car backfiring,' said Danny, while Chaz pulled a face at him.

Avoiding the lift, Chaz followed Danny as he ran up six flights of stairs and wandered along the corridor to Kelly's door.

'Hang on for Christ's sake, it's like being back in basic training hanging around with you,' said Chaz, breathing heavily.

'Come on, you're not going soft on me, are you?' Danny shouted behind him.

'Funny, that's what the wife said last night,' Chaz replied, chuckling.

The door opened and Kelly invited them in.

'Hi, Danny, long time no see. Oh hello, it's Charles, isn't it? I recognise you from Darren's Regiment pictures.'

'Yeah, it is. Just call me Chaz—everyone else does.'

'Sorry to bother you, Kelly love. Do you know where Darren is? We really need to find him,' said Danny, dispensing with small talk.

'Why, what's the little twat done now?'

'We're not sure, it might be something he did back in the Regiment,' said Danny, checking his watch.

'I'll give you his address but he won't be there, he'll be in The Feathers, down by the river on Church Walk. It's game night and he's on the darts team.'

Danny and Chaz said their goodbyes and

made their way downstairs. When they exited the stairwell on the ground floor, blue lights strobed their way through the glass foyer. They left the building, noticing the two injured youths had managed to drag themselves up and disappear. Heading towards the car, Danny and Chaz showed no interest in the police cars and armed officers milling about the place.

'Excuse me, gentlemen, may I have a word?'

'Certainly, officer. What can we do for you?' said Danny, upbeat and friendly.

'We've had a report of a gunshot. Have you heard or seen anything suspicious tonight?'

'Sorry, mate. We only popped in to see a friend, haven't seen or heard anything,' said Chaz with a disarming smile.

'Ok, thank you. Have a good evening.'

They gave the officer a nod and headed back to   the   car.

FOUR

The car park at The Feathers was packed. They entered the bar to find it crowded and in good spirits. Danny and Chaz squeezed themselves through the crowd toward the cheers and noise from the darts teams. Smudge finished his throw with a treble twenty and the team all yelled. He turned and grabbed his pint, spotting Danny and Chaz as he drained the glass.

'Oi, oi, muckers,' he shouted, throwing his arms in the air as he barged drunkenly through the crowd towards them.

Smudge threw his arms around them before grabbing Chaz either side of the face and kissing him on the forehead.

'I fucking love you guys,' he slurred, turning to

grab Danny.

'Yeah, yeah, we love you too, you big fucking idiot. Smudge, I need you to concentrate. We've got trouble, the old kind. From Zaidal,' said Danny, pushing his hands away as he watched Smudge sober to his word.

'What do you mean trouble from Zaidal?'

'Not here, let's go somewhere quiet,' said Danny leading them out of the pub.

'Let's go to mine, it's only down the road,' said Smudge with worried confusion written on his face.

Danny and Chaz followed him down the road to a small terrace house. They sat in his lounge while Smudge grabbed beers from the fridge.

'Right, what the fuck's going on?' he said chucking them a can each.

'Short version: a bunch of religious nuts from the mosque in Zaidal have got Fergus and are going to kill him unless they get some holy box containing ancient rosary beads back,' said Danny, looking accusingly at him.

'Oh,' said Smudge, his eyes looking guiltily between Danny and Chaz.

'Smudge, you stupid bastard. You and your

bloody souvenirs. Just tell us you still have it,' said Chaz, raising his voice to him.

'Eh, no. Look, the place was bombed out, I didn't think anyone would miss it. I'm sorry, ok?'

'Never mind that, we've gotta find that box or Fergus is done for. What did you do with it?' said Danny, forcing Smudge to focus.

'I sold it to Stavros, the Greek, about three months ago. He's got a dodgy antiques shop on Whitechapel Road; buys anything, no questions.'

'Right, first thing in the morning we'll go and see Stavros. How much did he give you for it?' said Danny.

'Three hundred quid, right result,' said Smudge breaking into a grin.

'A rare 15th century box containing some 9th century prophet's rosary beads. Three hundred quid. Smudge, you're a fucking idiot,' said Chaz shaking his head.

'Nah, just the box, I kept the beads. I thought they'd bring me luck.'

'Yeah, well how's that working out for you?' said Danny looking around the crappy little living room.

'Fuck me, nice to see you two wankers as well,' said Smudge opening a drawer in an old sideboard in the corner and pulling out the rosary beads.

Despite everything, it was good to see Smudge again, and no matter how angry they were with him, he still made them laugh.

'Well, one out of two is a good start,' said Danny taking the beads off him and putting them into his jacket pocket.

'You two wanna stay here the night? We can go straight to see Stavros first thing.'

'Ok, thanks, Smudge, and mate, it's good to see you too.'

Smudge grinned and pulled some takeout menus from the sideboard. 'What'll it be then, Chinese, Indian, pizza?'

FIVE

They were up early the next morning, crossing London in Danny's car. They drove past the infamous Blind Beggar pub where Ronnie Kray murdered George Cornell, and parked up in between a line of market traders' vans. The road was buzzing with a multi-cultural hive of activity as market traders from all walks of life set up their stalls for the day ahead. Chaz came back to the car with arms full of bacon rolls and coffee from Greggs. They sat in the car tucking in as they looked across at Stavros's closed shop.

'What time do you think he opens up?' said Chaz from the back seat.

'He's usually there by half eight,' said Smudge through a mouth full of bacon roll.

The other two looked at him, both thinking the same thing.

'Just how often do you deal with this guy, Smudge?' said Danny with a raised eyebrow.

'Now and then. What? Times are hard and work's thin on the ground. Sometimes he asks me to find things for him.'

'So you steal stuff,' said Chaz shaking his head.

'Don't fucking judge me, mate. The SAS was my life. Since I left, I can't even get a job in bloody McDonald's,' said Smudge, getting angry at his two mates.

'Alright, it's ok, none of us are perfect. We've all done stuff we're not proud of. Let's just concentrate on getting the box back and saving Fergus,' said Danny spotting a short, fat man with unmistakably Greek features approaching the antiques shop.

'Is that him? Stavros?'

The phone in Danny's pocket buzzed as he pointed at the Greek out the window.

'Yeah, that's Stavros,' said Smudge.

Danny looked at the message in front of him.

Tick tock, Mr Pearson.

'Let's go,' he said, throwing the car door open.

The shop looked like it had been around since Victorian days, coated in layers of peeling black gloss with gold gilt writing on the sign above the door. *Stavros Artino Antiques.*

Another sign on the door as they entered said '*Cash waiting for gold and silver*'. A brass bell on a spring above the door rang as its frame hit it on opening. Stavros appeared from out the back and greeted them from behind a glass counter full of old gold rings and chains and traded-in watches.

'Darren, how nice to see you. Who are your friends?' he said, his face all smiles as his eyes danced between Danny and Chaz nervously.

'This is Danny and Chaz. Listen, Stavy, you remember that fancy box I sold you a couple of months ago? We need it back, mate, no bullshit. It's a matter of life and death,' said Smudge stepping forward.

'Darren, my friend, I do not have it.'

'Look, I haven't got time to fuck about. Where's the box?' said Danny, his face set in stone and his eyes staring, dark and menacing.

'I sold it to a collector,' Stavros said backing

away from the counter a foot or so to distance himself from Danny.

'Tell us who, we'll buy it back. How much did you get for it? Four, five hundred?' said Smudge trying to keep the conversation light.

'Eh, he won't sell it to you.'

'What? Why? How much did you sell it for?' repeated Smudge.

'Twenty-five thousand pounds.'

'What? You fucking slippery, scheming bastard! Three hundred fucking quid he gave me. I'll fucking kill him,' growled Smudge, slamming his fist down on the counter.

'Who's got the box?' shouted Danny, silencing the shop.

'William Henson.'

'Please tell me you didn't sell it to William 'Hatchet' Henson?' said Smudge, suddenly looking worried as Stavros nodded.

'Will someone tell me who the fuck William 'Hatchet' Henson is?' said Danny angrily, his patience running thin.

'He runs most of south London. Extortion, prostitution, drug dealing... You name it, he's got his fingers into it. People who cross him tend to lose limbs, hence 'Hatchet' Henson,' said Smudge to Danny and Chaz.

'I don't care if he's the fucking pope, Fergus's life's on the line and we need that box. So how are we going to get it?' said Chaz, refocusing the group.

'We'll have to bust into his gaff and take it,' said Danny, ready for action.

'Whoa, hold on, Big Bollocks, this guy's a serious player. He lives in a big house in Wimbledon, behind a big wall, electric gates and tooled-up thugs,' said Smudge.

'Not to mention he keeps his antiques in a steel-lined strong room with a combination-locked door,' said Stavros chipping in.

'Well, that's just fucking great. Anything else we should know about—gun turrets, a bloody minefield?' said Chaz pacing about.

'There may be a way,' said Stavros, silencing the group as all eyes fell on him.

'Go on,' they said in unison.

'I know a man who can get you into that room, but it will cost much money, my friends,' said Stavros, pausing to let his words sink in.

'Well, that's us screwed then. We don't have

any money,' said Smudge, throwing his hands in the air.

'Well, maybe we could help each other?'

'Go on,' they said again.

'I would be willing to finance this little venture,' said Stavros, a wide grin spreading across his face.

'And why would you do that?' said Danny, not liking the way Stavros had manipulated the conversation.

'There is something in that room I desire. If you get it for me, I will get you whatever you need—plans of the house, equipment—and I will get the man to get you into that room. The rest is up to you.'

Danny looked at the others, already knowing they had no choice. Fergus's life depended on them and they would do anything to get him back. Smudge and Chaz nodded their agreement back, and Danny turned to Stavros.

'What do you want from the room?'

'There is an oil painting of two sisters sitting on a terrace with a lake in the background. It is hung above the desk in that room. I get you in, you get the painting for me and the box for yourselves,' said Stavros, enjoying the upper hand as he exploited their situation.

'Ok, but we have to do this today,' said Danny, leaning in. His face turning as hard as granite and his eyes boring into him, unnervingly dark and dangerous.

The smile vanished from Stavros's face 'Today? I would need more time. Today is too soon. I—'

'Today,' growled Danny again.

'Ok, ok, come back in two hours. I will see what I can do.'

SIX

The three of them left Stavros's shop. They hurried over and jumped into the car, roaring off before an approaching traffic warden could give them a ticket. After finding a car park they walked into the nearest café. They got drinks and found a table away from other customers.

'Ok, what do you think?' said Danny to Chaz and Smudge.

'I can't lie, I don't like the timeframe,' said Chaz.

'Who does? But we don't have a choice. Can we trust Stavros to come good, Smudge?' said Danny, falling back into his old role as team leader.

'Yes, guv, I know Stavros. If he wants the

painting in that room, he's been planning on getting it for a long time.'

'Good, so we go with it. We figure a way of getting Henson out of the house and then go in and get the box and the painting out. Only the box and the painting, Smudge. No souvenirs, ok? I'm not going through this again,' said Danny, managing a chuckle at Smudge's expense.

'Yeah, yeah, I get it,' replied Smudge, accepting his verbal punishment.

'Tell us what you know about Hatchet Henson, Smudge.'

'Erm, he grew up in the shit end of Fulham, rising up from petty crime to a major player. He got his nickname when a rival killed his brother. Henson tracked him down, dragging him out of his local boozer. They found most of his hacked-up body in the Thames, the suspected weapon a small hatchet axe. Since then there's been no stopping him. He's mostly legit nowadays, ploughing his ill-gotten gains into property, clubs, pubs and antiques. He's still a dangerous little fucker though.'

'Mm, what about family?' said Danny deep in

thought.

'Er, a wife, Marian, and a daughter in her early twenties, Jessica, I think. She works in Henson's Wimbledon property letting agencies. What you thinking, boss?'

'We need something to get them out of the house while we go in,' said Danny draining the last of his tea.

'Why don't we grab the daughter and phone Henson up, tell him she's been in an accident and is at, I don't know, the Royal London Hospital in Whitechapel. That'd give us an hour or so while they drive there, find out it's bollocks and drive back,' said Chaz thinking out loud.

'Yeah that could work, good thinking, Charlie boy. Come on, let's get back to Stavros's.'

They left the car in the car park and walked back to Stavros's shop. Whitechapel Road was busy with the market stalls all set up and people milling about. There was nowhere to park and London's traffic wardens appeared to have ninja training as they materialised out of nowhere to slap tickets on the windscreens of the chancers who'd risk parking illegally. They entered the antiques shop, its door knocking the little brass bell above it to announce their arrival. Stavros appeared from out back with a short, fat man; he was like a carbon copy of Stavros, but with no hair.

'This is my cousin Nikko. He can get you into the strong room,' said Stavros beaming from ear to ear.

'So when you say you're going to finance the mission you really mean you're going to bung your cousin a few quid,' said Chaz rather disgruntled.

'What? You want into the room, I get you into the room,' said Stavros shrugging.

'Right everyone, zip it. Stavros, what have you got for us?' said Danny, raising his voice.

'Ok, I have a plan of the house. Nikko has a frequency scanner that will open the gates. You will have to get him into the house but once in, he can disarm the alarm and get you into the strong room.'

'How can he get us into the room?' said Danny, pushing the point further.

'It's no problem. I have to drill into the framework and bypass the lock, popping it open,' said Nikko grinning like Stavros next to him.

Danny didn't like Nikko and Stavros's amateur-hour plan. It wouldn't normally get a look in, but time was short and they didn't have any other choices.

'Chaz, Smudge, you good?' said Danny, seeking their united approval.

They both nodded back at him.

'Right, we're good. Stavros, I need two grand for supplies. Nikko, be ready, we'll pick you up later this afternoon,' said Danny picking up the plans of Henson's house and turning to leave.

'Two thousand, what for?'

'That's my business. If you want that painting I need two grand,' said Danny with a look not to be argued with.

'Mm, ok. What time will you be back?' said Stavros, pulling a fat roll of notes from his trouser pocket.

'Fuck me, you could buy a small country with that,' said Smudge, raising his eyebrows.

'As soon as I've figured out how to get Henson out of the house. Just be ready we may not have much time. Ok?' said Danny, ignoring Smudge while taking the money.

Stavros and Nikko both nodded in agreement. With the plan in motion, Danny, Smudge and Chaz turned and left the shop.

SEVEN

'We need some untraceable wheels that don't lead back to us, Smudge.' said Danny as they walked through the hustle and shouts of traders along Whitechapel Road.

'Oh lovely, why do you think I'd know where to get a bent motor?' said Smudge looking offended.

'Do you?' questioned Danny.

'Well yes, but you shouldn't just assume I do.'

'Shut up, you prat,' chuckled Danny.

Back in the car, Danny followed Smudge's directions to a tatty garage tucked under the railway arches in Hackney. It was the kind of garage you'd go to to buy a car because you desperately needed one and couldn't get credit anywhere else.

The M4 gurgled to a halt in front of the row of cars for sale ranging from £200 to £1800, all in varying states of tattiness.

'Jesus, I think I overdid the money from Stavros,' said Danny climbing out of the car.

Hearing them approach, a big middle-aged guy in greasy blue overalls walked to the open roller door wiping his hands on a rag. He had a face that looked like it had gone ten rounds with Mike Tyson, and was obviously an ex-boxer. He eyed Danny and Chaz with suspicion before zeroing in on Smudge.

'Alright, Phil?' said Smudge unusually apprehensive.

'£500 now,' Phil said, clearly annoyed.

'Hold tight, Phil, no need for agro. I've got your money, and money for another deal.'

'Money first.'

Smudge glanced across at Danny who got the hint and peeled off £500 of Stavros's money.

'Ok, Phil, we good?' said Smudge handing him the money.

He counted it slowly, making them wait. When he was satisfied, he folded the notes in half and tucked them in his overall pocket.

'What do you want?' he finally said.

'We need a car, nothing special. False plates, no papers. Untraceable.'

'Who are these two?' said Phil, caution returning.

'They're old friends of mine. They're totally sound, I'd stake my life on it.'

'You just did,' he said gruffly. He looked left and right before cocking his head for them to follow him inside.

As soon as they entered, Phil lowered the roller door behind them. He dragged a sheet off a dayglow orange Ford Transit van.

'What the fuck is that?' said Smudge in surprise.

'It's an ex-Dyno Rod van, and it's all I got. It's taxed and MOT'd and registered to some guy who just got sent down for a ten stretch. £800 and I've never seen the van and I've never seen you,' said Phil with a definite take it or fuck off attitude.

'It's not exactly inconspicuous is it? It's hurting my fucking eyes. Look at it,' said Smudge screwing up his face at it.

'We'll take it,' said Danny counting out the cash, his patience wearing thin.

Phil took the money and threw them the keys before rolling the shutter door back up. Danny gave the keys to Smudge, who took them grudgingly.

'You follow us back to mine, I'll drop the car off and we'll head for Henson's, picking up Nikko on the way.'

'Agh, fuck's sake. Why have I gotta drive this piece of shit?' said Smudge, grumbling.

'Because you're the fucking idiot who caused this mess, now shut up and drive the van,' said an annoyed Danny while Chaz stood beside him shaking his head.

Smudge stood for a sec dumbfounded before shrugging and getting in the van mumbling to himself.

'Jesus, you make one mistake and nobody ever lets you forget it.'

They dropped Danny's car off and went for Nikko, stopping on the way to get a box of latex gloves, overalls and masks from a fancy dress shop. Danny googled Wimbledon property lets as they drove before making a call.

'Hi, could I speak to Jessica please?' he said, waiting for a second while they transferred him.

'Jessica speaking,' came a bright and bubbly voice.

'Hi, Jessica. A friend of mine said to give you a call. I'm very interested in the five-bed property you have in Seymore Road.'

'Ah yes, that property is still available, Mr...?'

'Mr Whitmore. The thing is, Jessica, I'm only in London for the next couple of hours. I have to fly out to Dubai later this afternoon and would really love it if you could show me the property before I go,' said Danny trying to sound as businesslike as possible.

'Eh, I could shuffle a few things around and meet you at the house at say two o'clock.'

'Perfect. Thank you, Jessica, I will see you then,' said Danny hanging up and smiling at the boys.

'Right, we grab the daughter at the house, tie her up and leave her at the property. They'll go looking for her after a couple of hours, by which time we'll be long gone. We take her phone and make the call to Daddy, he speeds off to the hospital and we're in and out before anyone's any the wiser.'

'Roger that. Hang in there, Fergus, we're coming for you, mate,' said Chaz, to the other two's approval.

At quarter-to-two they parked the glaring van down the street from the rental house. With overalls and masks and armed with gaffer tape, they watched and waited for Jessica to arrive.

EIGHT

At one forty-five a Mini Cooper pulled up to the house. A pretty blonde got out and totted along on high heels with a clipboard to the front door. She fumbled with a big bunch of keys before finding the right one and opening it.

'Right, mask on, Smudge, let's go,' said Chaz pulling his mask down over his face.

'Why did you have to pick clowns? I fucking hate clowns,' moaned Smudge pulling his one down.

'That's funny, considering you are one,' said Chaz, pushing him out the van door.

They looked either way and scooted across the road. Without stopping, they flew into the house. Chaz grabbed Jessica from behind, clamping a hand over her mouth.

'Grab her legs,' he shouted to Smudge.

As Smudge moved round her she bit into Chaz's hand hard.

'Agh, fuck!' said Chaz letting go just as Smudge moved in front of her. Screaming like a banshee, Jessica kicked Smudge in the balls.

'Agh, fuck!' shouted Smudge grabbing his family jewels.

Seizing the moment, she turned and legged it to the door. Still screaming, she threw it open only to be met by Danny in a clown mask and boiler suit. Caught by surprise, Danny reacted on impulse and punched her between the eyes, knocking her flat on her back, out cold.

'Shit,' he said stepping inside and closing the door as Chaz and Smudge appeared in the hallway.

'What the fuck are you two playing at? All you had to do was tie her up.'

'She's tougher than she looks,' said Smudge, struggling to stand upright.

Chaz stopped shaking his hand where Jessica had bitten through his latex glove. He grabbed her arms while Danny grabbed her legs. They took her through to the lounge and taped her arms and legs together. After placing a final piece of tape over her mouth, they put her in the cupboard under the stairs. Danny placed her thumb on her phone to unlock it. He found the Mum and Dad home contact and called it.

'Hello?' came a gruff male voice.

'Is this Mr Henson?'

'Who's asking?' came a cautious voice in return.

'Mr Henson, this is Doctor White at the Royal London Hospital, Whitechapel. Your daughter's been involved in a serious car accident,' Danny said in his most formal voice.

'What, Jessica? Is she ok?'

'She's going into theatre now. It may be a good idea for you and your wife to get down here.'

'Ok, we're on our way. Thank you, Doctor,' Henson said hanging up.

Danny put the phone in Jessica's bag, chucking it in the cupboard with her before closing the door.

'That's it. Let's go,' he said leading the way out of the house.

Inside the cupboard, Jessica's eyes flicked open. From the slither of light under the door she figured out she was in a cupboard. After growing up in her father's footsteps she wasn't scared; rage and frustration took over as she lay on her back and kicked repeatedly at the door as hard as she could. Outside, Danny and the group drove off in the dayglow orange van, heading for Henson's house.

NINE

Forty metres down the road from the Henson home, in a plain Ford Escort, sat undercover detectives Miles Green and Karl Leonard. The dash was awash with snack wrappers and empty coffee cups. They'd been on reconnaissance at the Hensons' house for three days now, gaining intelligence on his known associates.

'Hello, gates are opening,' said Miles, glad of the activity to break the monotony.

Seconds later, Henson and his wife sped out in their Mercedes followed by two of his thugs in a four-by-four. They sped off down the road and out of sight in seconds.

'Bloody hell, he's in a hurry,' said Karl.

'Yeah, I guess we might as well call it a day,'

replied Miles.

'I suppose— hold up, what's this?' said Karl watching the dayglow van roll up to the gate.

The side door opened and a short, fat guy in a boiler suit and clown mask stuck his arm out and pointed something at the gate, causing it to swing open slowly. The door slid shut and the driver looked up and down the street in another clown mask before driving up the drive. The gates slid smoothly shut behind it.

'What shall we do, call it in?'

'And say what? A bunch of clowns have turned up in a luminous orange van? Nah, let's wait and see what happens,' said Miles.

***

Inside the gates, Danny took the front door out with one massive swing of a ten-pound hammer. Nikko moved in and disarmed the security alarm before waving them in. They carried Nikko's kit bags inside, moving to one side of the stairs where the plans said the strong room was.

'Where's the bloody door then?' said Smudge, running his hands around the floor-to-ceiling bookshelves lining the hall.

'It's here somewhere. There must be a false bit in the shelves or a hidden door. Look for a catch,' said Danny, pulling books out of the way.

'Got it,' said Chaz pushing a tucked away button.

A hinged section of the bookshelf clicked forward. Pulling it open exposed a solid, locked metal door with an electronic keypad on one side.

'You're up, Nikko. How long will it take?' said Danny through his mask.

'Eh, ten, maybe fifteen minutes,' said Nikko, clicking a large drill onto a tripod and sliding it into place.

'Ok. Chaz, keep an eye out front. Smudge, don't touch anything,' said Danny eyeing him looking around the living room.

'I'm not. Jeez, gimme a break.'

***

Two miles away in the cupboard, Jessica had kicked a football-sized hole in the door. As the light came in she rolled towards her bag.

Managing to get herself into a sitting position, she fumbled with her hands tied behind her until she got her fingers on the zip. After five minutes of struggling, she got it open and rooted around inside. She flinched as she pricked her finger on the little pair of scissors she was looking for. Flicking them open, she screwed her wrists up and nibbled away at the gaffer tape with the blade. Eventually it cut enough for her to snap free. She peeled off the gag and delved back in the bag for her phone and made a call.

'Dad, I need help. Some bastard punched me out and tied me up.'

'Jessy, what? But the accident, the hospital!' he yelled over the sound of the speeding car.

'What you talking about, Dad? I ain't been in no accident and I ain't in no fucking hospital. I'm in the rental on Seymore Road.'

'Fuck! It's a trick to get me out of the house. You get yourself out of there, princess. I'll deal with this,' Henson shouted over the sound of screeching brakes.

***

Nikko's drill screeched and smoked as it cut slowly through the stainless steel lining of the strong room. Danny paced up and down looking at his watch way too often as the seconds ticked by excruciatingly slowly. Finally there was a ping and Nikko turned the drill off. Pulling it back out of the way, he exposed a smoking hole in the blue-black discoloured steel panel.

'All good, Nikko?' said Danny, picking up the drill and passing it to Smudge to put back in the van.

'Yes, good, give me a couple of minutes and we'll be in,' said Nikko sliding the clown mask up on top of his head and grinning like a Cheshire cat.

He got a flexible inspection camera with a pair of cutters attached to the end. Sliding it into the hole, he watched the screen as he slid the end deeper into the frame. The electronic lock and its coloured loom of wires suddenly filled the tiny screen. Nikko eased it around until the tiny jaws hooked around the red wire. He squeezed the scissor-like handles, pulling the cutters closed and snipping the wire. The lock let out a continuous buzzing noise as Nikko manipulated the gadget onto another wire. With all eyes on him he snipped again. The buzzing sound stopped and the lock clicked, pinging the door open a couple of inches.

'Abracadabra,' he said, still grinning.

'Top man,' said Danny slapping Nikko on the back as they pulled the door wide open.

TEN

Danny stepped into the room, spotting the painting as it hung on the wall facing him. His face fell as his eyes moved to the shelf below.

'Smudge, get your arse in here.'

'What's up?' said Smudge, entering the small room.

Danny moved to one side so he could see the shelf.

'Fuck me,' said Smudge, staring at the dozen or so antique boxes in front of him.

'Please tell me you know which one is our box.'

'Yeah, er. Just give me a minute,' said Smudge, shuffling through the boxes.

'Smudge, we don't have a minute. We've

gotta move,' said Danny, looking at his watch before lifting down the painting.

'I need more time. It's got a mark inside where the beads discoloured the bottom,' Smudge said, frantically opening the lids.

'Fuck it, we've gotta move. Take the lot. You can go through them in the van,' said Danny handing the picture to Nikko and grabbing an armful of boxes.

Smudge did the same and headed for the van.

'What the fuck's this, a Tupperware party?' said Chaz scratching his head as they came out.

'Never mind that, just get the van started, Chaz,' shouted Danny, shutting Smudge and Nikko in the back with the stuff. He hopped in the front as Chaz rolled closer to the gates. The sensor picked them up, triggering the gates to swing smoothly open. All eyes went wide at the sight of Henson driving like a lunatic towards them in his Mercedes, with his paid muscle following in a blacked-out four-by-four.

'Fucking floor it, Chaz! Go, go, go!'

Stamping his foot to the floor, the old van lurched forward in a cloud of diesel smoke. Chaz aimed straight at Henson who swerved to the side at the last minute, his face a picture of rage as his eyes met clown masks before the cars whizzed past each other. The no-necked muscle driving behind Henson swerved too late and the van slammed into the rear corner, spinning it round behind as it roared past.

***

'Get out, Marian, my love. Put the kettle on, I'll be back in a jiffy,' said Henson, his face going calm. He reached past her and pulled a Glock 17 handgun out of the glove box.

'Alright, Bill, hurry up and kill the little bastards. Remember, we've got reservations at The Ivy tonight.'

'Ok, treacle, I won't be long,' he said as his men abandoned their wrecked car and climbed into the Merc. As the doors shut, Henson's face contorted into anger once more. Smoke poured off the tyres as the wheels spun the powerful car after the dayglow van.

***

In the parked Ford Escort, a sausage roll in one hand and tea in a polystyrene cup in the other, Miles and Karl stared out in disbelief at the carnage unfolding in front of them.

'Shit, bloody hell,' cursed Miles, starting the engine and spilling hot tea all over his lap.

Karl threw his half-eaten sausage roll in the back and grabbed the radio.

'Control from Whisky Five Five, over.'

'Whisky Five Five, go ahead, over,'

'Requesting armed response unit. We are in pursuit of a Silver Mercedes S350 belonging to William Henson. He is in pursuit of a bright orange Ford Transit van suspected of a burglary at his premises. Suspects are heading east on A238 towards the A24 at Colliers Wood. The occupants of the Mercedes and possibly the Transit are armed,' Karl shouted down the radio as he slung the remnants of his tea out the window.

'Whisky Five Five, backup and armed response unit are on their way, over.'

***

'Agh, fuck's sake, Chaz,' shouted Smudge as he rolled around in the back of the van, frantically trying to hold on to antique boxes as he tried to find the right one.

'Hold on, Smudge, we've got company,' said Chaz, eyeing the fast approaching Mercedes in the wing mirror.

'We'll never lose them in this tub of shit. Whoa,' said Danny as the passenger mirror exploded into tiny pieces.

***

'Tony, shoot the fucking tyres, not the bloody mirror, you twat,' Henson shouted as Tony hung out the window trying to aim his gun as the car snaked wildly about.

He shot again as Henson hit a pothole, sending the bullet wildly off target.

***

'Shit!' yelled Smudge as a bullet burst through the rear door, blasting the box he was looking at out of his hand.

'Please tell me that wasn't our box,' said Danny looking back.

'Nah, we're good,' replied Smudge sliding across the back to grab another box.

'Do something!' yelled Nikko, his eyes wide and face pale.

Danny's phone rang as they slid sideways round a corner.

'What?' he shouted without looking at the ID.

'Time is running out and so is my patience, Mr Pearson. My brothers will kill Mr McKinsey if we don't get our prop—'

'We've got your box, I'll call you back,' said Danny hanging up as another bullet popped through the back door, exiting in a neat round circle through the front windscreen.

'I've got it, this is the box,' yelled Smudge from the back.

'You sure?' said Danny, turning to look at him over the seat.

'Yep, positive.'

'Get us out of here, Chaz,' Danny said, turning to Chaz in the driving seat.

'Hold tight, I've got an idea,' Chaz shouted over the screaming engine.

ELEVEN

'Boss, there's a car chasing us,' said Tony, glaring out the back window of the Merc.

'Fuck me, has somebody been handing out party invites? Fire a couple off at him, scare the wanker off.'

***

'Is this as fast as this thing goes?' said Karl in the undercover police car.

'I'm giving it all it's got. Hello, what's Henson's bloke doing out the window? Oh shit, get down!' shouted Miles as bullets sparked off the car's bodywork.

Karl grabbed the radio. 'Whisky Five Five to

control, we need the armed backup now. We are under fire, I repeat we are under fire.'

'Control to Whisky Five Five, be advised to back off. Armed response ETA two minutes.'

'Roger that. Whisky Five Five standing down.'

'Give it up, Miles, let the heavy mob take over,' said Karl to Miles who let his foot off the gas, letting the Merc pull away from them.

***

'I hear sirens, Chaz. Whatever you're planning, do it quick,' shouted Danny.

'It's just up ahead.'

'What is?' said Danny, clueless.

'There's a pedestrian walkway under the railway line leading to my nan's estate.'

'So?'

'So get ready to run. It's a right warren. We'll hide up at nan's and leave when it quiets down,' said Chaz with a grin.

'How we going to stop them following?'

'Here it comes, hold tight.'

The road ahead turned to follow a high embankment with train lines to the city centre on top. Below it was the concrete passage of the walkway to the estate. Chaz bounced up the kerb with a jolt that felt like the front wheels would come off. He handbrake-turned the van so it faced the Merc and Henson closing fast. Grinding the van into reverse, Chaz floored it, sending them hurtling backwards to the entrance of the walkway. Danny could see Henson's enraged, bright red face getting closer as Chaz struck the V-shaped entrance. The van echoed with a horrific metal scraping sound as it wedged itself into the opening.

'Right, out the back doors, go, go, go,' shouted Chaz already halfway over the front seat.

They leaped out into the walkway. Danny looked through the van and out the windscreen before slamming the back doors shut. Henson's Merc bounced up the kerb, closely followed by a convoy of police vehicles closing in behind him, sirens wailing.

Clicking the key fob to lock the van and effectively seal off the walkway, Danny turned and ran after Chaz and Smudge and Nikko. They came out in the centre of the concrete jungle of 1950s blocks of flats.

'Come on, boys, it's at least a five-minute drive to the nearest road under the tracks and back, and they ain't getting that van out of the passage any time soon.'

They followed Chaz through the estate which was thankfully quiet in the late afternoon. Ducking into a stairwell, they took off the masks and gloves and followed Chaz up to a third-floor flat. After a couple of rings, a little old lady answered the door.

'Oh hello, Charlie, Danny, lovely to see you. Oh, is that you, Darren? I haven't seen you for ages. How are you? Come in, come in,' she said, leaving the door open and walking off to the kitchen.

'We're good, Mrs Leman,' said Danny, taking a quick look each way before closing the front door and shutting out the sound of sirens from the other side of the railway tracks.

'Go sit down. You boys want tea?' she said, rattling cups out of the cupboard.

'Yes please, Nan. You got a bin bag?' said Chaz.

'What do you want that for, Charlie?'

'We've been decorating Smudge's flat and

want to get out of these overalls. We don't want to get dirt on your sofa, do we, boys?'

They all murmured their agreement and started unzipping and sliding out of them. She came back in with a tray of cups and a bin bag, then went back out into the kitchen to fetch a freshly made Victoria sponge cake.

'Help yourselves, boys, you look like you've worked up an appetite.'

'Thanks, Mrs Leman.'

She sat down with them, looking at Smudge holding the gold box and Nikko with a two-foot-by-two-foot painting.

'You been out bargain hunting, loves?' she said casually.

'Er, yes, Mrs Leman. As Chaz said, I'm sprucing up my flat. Got these from a garage sale in Wimbledon.'

'I like that box, Darren, I could keep my earrings in that,' she chuckled.

They stayed for over an hour before leaving separately. Nikko went first with the painting for Stavros, then Smudge and Danny left with the timekeeper's box. Finally, Chaz gave his nan a kiss on the cheek before following a couple of minutes behind. There were only a few police wandering the estate. After arresting Henson and his men for firearms offences, they assumed the four guys in boiler suits and clown masks had fled the scene directly after the van crash. They paid Danny, Smudge and Chaz no attention as they left separately. Chaz dumped the bin bag of overalls and masks in a large commercial bin behind a garage a safe distance from the estate. The three of them met up outside the Tube station about a mile from the estate. Danny took out his phone and made a call before they entered.

'We have the box. Be at my house in 30 minutes with Fergus.'

'Very well, Mr Pearson, we will see y—'

Danny hung up before Hasan finished talking.

TWELVE

Chaz and Danny checked the road outside his house several times before entering. All was quiet. They stood side by side in the lounge, staring out the window at the quiet suburban road outside. Although the wait was short, the tension was insufferable. Danny counted the seconds away by the rhythmic beat of his heart, which he could feel banging away in his chest. Dead on thirty minutes from his call, two cars pulled up outside. Hasan plus three similar-looking Syrians stepped out of the front vehicle. They walked confidently to the front door and stopped without knocking.

Danny made them wait a few seconds just because he felt like it. Finally, he moved to the door and clicked it open, letting it swing inward as he walked away to the lounge. Hasan entered, looking calm and relaxed. His men followed him and fanned out in the room, trying their best to look tough and intimidating.

'You have our property,' said Hasan, getting straight to it.

'Where's Fergus first?' said Danny, his eyes boring into Hasan's, dark and dangerous.

Hasan put his phone to his ear and spoke in Arabic while pointing out the front window. All heads turned to see the car behind lowering the rear window. Fergus's face was pushed into view. He looked tired and bruised, but otherwise ok.

'Enough is enough, Mr Pearson, where is our box?'

This time Chaz put his phone to his ear. 'Bring it in, Smudge.'

They waited in silence, the room remaining tense, like gunslingers waiting to draw. All eyes darted to all eyes, waiting for the catalyst to end the deadlock. Finally, the back door opened. Smudge walked in and looked at Danny, who nodded the ok. Reaching inside his jacket, he pulled out the ornate 15th century box that had once belonged to Mohammad Al-Hamawi. Hasan took it carefully from him. He opened it and looked upon the great prophet Elijah's rosary beads. The four of them murmured a prayer chant in Arabic before Hasan shut the box and looked at Danny.

'This matter is now closed, Mr Pearson. We are men of faith, not radicals or revengeful extremists. Your friend Mr McKinsey is free to go,' said Hasan, handing his phone to the man beside him. He spoke in Arabic as Danny, Chaz and Smudge watched the front passenger of the car outside climb out and open the rear door. He pulled a knife and leaned in, cutting the cable ties free from Fergus's ankles and wrists. When Danny turned back to Hasan, he and his men were already leaving. He watched them pass Fergus without looking at him and get back in their car. They moved off a second later, leaving Fergus by the kerb. He walked up the path and entered the front door.

'Alright losers? Which one of you tossers have I got to thank for the weekend break with the fun bunch then?' said Fergus, giving a hug and slap on the back to each of them.

'That was my fault, sorry, Fergus,' said Smudge, backing away sheepishly.

'Yeah, I fucking thought it might be. This is going to cost you a shitload of beer to make up for this,' said Fergus, dropping the serious face for a grin.

'I can do better than that,' said Smudge, putting his hand in his pocket and pulling out a bunch of expensive watches. 'How about a Roly, Ferg, or a Breitling?'

'Smudge, where did you get that lot from?' said Danny, already suspecting the answer.

'What can I say? They were just sitting there in Henson's strong room. He's not going to need them, doing a ten stretch for possessing a firearm,' said Smudge with a cheeky grin.

'First, I want a beer. Then you can tell me what the hell's been going on, and who the fuck Henson is,' said Fergus, puzzled.

'Beer I can do,' said Danny, heading for the fridge. When he came back in, he threw a can to each of them. When they'd all cracked them open, he held his up in a toast. 'Alpha team,' he said to his SAS brothers-in-arms.

'Alpha team,' the others said raising their cans.

The Book Signing

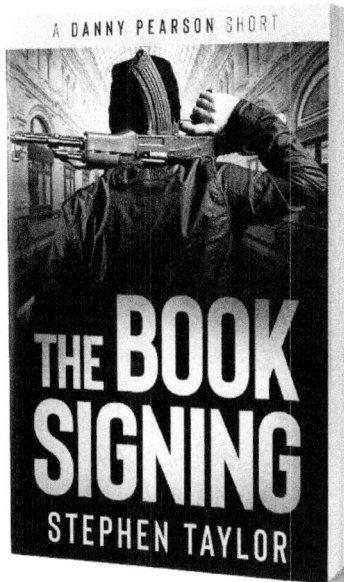

ONE

'So tell me again, old boy, why are we heading down Oxford Street instead of sitting in the Dog and Duck with a pint and a pub lunch?' said Danny's oldest and closest friend, Scott Miller.

'Plenty of time for that, Scotty boy. An old friend from the Regiment is doing a book signing at Harrington's department store. I haven't seen him for years and just want to say hello,' said Danny, weaving through London's busiest shopping street.

'OK, I suppose lunch can wait awhile. What's he written anyway? If he's anything like you, it'll be a colouring book with a pack of crayons,' said Scott, chuckling to himself.

'You're hilarious, Scott. You ever thought of

doing stand-up?' Danny said sarcastically.

'Well?' Scott insisted.

'Well what?' Danny said over his shoulder as he pushed through the entrance door to the grand old four-storey department store that was built in 1910 by the wealthy Harrington family in competition to Selfridges.

'Well, what has the blasted fellow written?' Scott said, running out of patience.

'It's a book about his time in the Middle East and his personal struggle afterwards. His unit spent months tracking and killing the terrorist Abdullahi Ash-Sharm.'

'What, the man who organised the rocket attack on the Houses of Parliament a few years back?' said Scott, suddenly interested.

'The very same, but what you won't have heard is the men who took him out were hit by a rocket launcher as they evacuated the area. Their armoured personnel carrier was destroyed. Mark was the only one to survive, just. He lost a leg, among other injuries, and is lucky to be alive.'

'Oh, I see. Well, eh, good for him,' said Scott, feeling a little awkward for taking the piss.

They moved through the perfume and makeup section of the shop and stopped by the escalators as Danny read the store guide positioned under a large hanging poster.

'That's a rather nice little trinket,' said Scott, admiring the picture of an exquisite diamond necklace with the heading, *"La Perfection Mouawad necklace on display in Harrington's jewellery department tonight at six."*

'I don't think even you could afford that one, mate,' said Danny, looking back at the store guide.

'Most definitely not. I read about it the other day. They lent it to princess someone or other for a royal bash and it's only on display here today before going back to Switzerland. I think the article said it was worth thirty-five million.'

'Is that all? I'll have two then. The book department's on the third floor,' chuckled Danny.

As he turned to look at Scott, a flick of nervous eye contact caught his eye from a Middle Eastern man shuffling through the crowd of shoppers in the direction of the front doors. Danny stood stock still, watching him as he moved through the perfume and makeup section.

Everything about the man was wrong, the way he moved, his head down, the little jerky movements as he looked around the store, the padded jacket in summer, and large rucksack strapped tightly to his back. When the man stopped in the middle of the makeup aisle, Danny tensed his legs, getting ready to move and raise the alarm. Everything about the man screamed suicide bomber. To his relief, two more Middle Eastern-looking guys with jackets and rucksacks approached and greeted the man. He smiled and the three of them headed off, disappearing out of sight through the main doors.

Tourists. Backpackers, I suppose. Christ, I must be losing my touch.

'I say, Earth to Daniel, are we going to this book signing or not?' said Scott, getting fed up with dodging the shoppers trying to get past him to the escalators.

'What? Eh, sorry, Scott. Yes, let's go,' Danny said, his attention back to Scott, the Middle Eastern guy forgotten as they headed up the escalator.

After zigzagging up the escalators between floors, they floated onto the third floor to see the book department expanding out ahead of them. Looking between customers browsing and a few small groups wandering about with signed copies of Mark Fairbanks's book under their arms, Danny spotted his friend sitting behind a desk loaded with his books. Mark looked a hundred times better than the last time Danny saw him. He was relaxed and tanned and had a full beard covering most of the scars on his face and neck. Mark handed a signed book back to a fan. He spotted Danny and Scott as the woman moved away, and beckoned them over.

'Danny! Good to see you, mate,' Mark said, pushing himself upright onto his prosthetic legs and extending a scarred hand missing its little finger.

'Good to see you as well, mate. The writer's life certainly seems to suit you,' Danny said, shaking Mark's hand.

'Well, it certainly beats the shit out of lying in a ditch up to you neck in muck and bullets,' Mark said, grinning back and looking across at

Scott.

'Sorry, Mark, this is my friend, Scott Miller,' Danny said, turning to introduce him.

'Hi Scott. Er, you're the computer geek, yeah?' said Mark, moving with a slight rocking motion as he walked forward to shake Scott's hand.

'Not my favourite term, old boy, but I guess you could call me that,' said Scott without taking offence.

'Danny used to talk about you all the time in the Regiment.'

'Really? All good things I hope,' said Scott, chuffed at being the central topic of conversation.

'Well, nearly all good,' Mark joked. 'Listen, I've got about ten minutes left with this lot then I'm free if you guys want to hang around?' said Mark, moving back behind the table as a man approached with his book for signing.

'Yeah, of course. We were going for lunch if you want to join us,' said Danny, standing to one side to let people through.

'Great, love to,' Mark said, looking at the man in front of him as he expressed his admiration for Mark's book.

'Can you make it out to Leonard please?' the man said.

'Leonard, sure, no problem.'

TWO

The three Middle Eastern men came back into the store through the main door. They stood just inside for a while, their hoods up to cover their throat mics and earpieces.

'This is Yanni, we're in position,' came the voice over the earpiece.

'This is Shan, we are in position, Yahid.'

'This is Karam, in position.'

'This is Omar, we are on the first floor.'

Twenty metres away, a Harrington's security guard reached for his radio, his eyes staying glued to the three suspicious hooded men at the entrance.

'Hey, this is Doug. I might need some help down here. I've got some suspicious looking characters, padded coats and rucksacks. It might be those animal rights lot we had last month, you know, the ones that chained themselves to the makeup stands over animal testing in cosmetics.'

The second Doug clicked off the radio, Yahid Ash-Sharm flicked his hood back and unzipped his jacket.

'Continue as planned, brothers,' he said, swinging up an MP5 submachine gun that hung over his shoulder. The two men beside him threw off their backpacks and unzipped their jackets, throwing them to the ground to leave their tactical vests, handguns, knives and MP5s exposed for all the confused shoppers and staff to see. Spotting Doug's podgy middle-aged body standing terrified to the spot, Yahid pulled the trigger and let off a quick burst of automatic fire, blowing Doug back into a makeup stand. The women on the counter beside him screamed as lipsticks and eyeliners rolled around the floor before stopping in a spreading puddle of sticky blood. Turning his gun, Yahid cut down two more counter staff.

'Everyone leave NOW!' Yahid shouted, turning away from them dismissively to focus on the other two men as they pulled chains and explosives from their rucksacks. In the distance, they could hear more gunshots as Yahid's men ushered people out of the store's alternative exit doors.

Panicking customers screamed, pushing, and trampling over each other as they crowded out onto Oxford Street. Gunfire echoed from the first floor, followed by a wave of customers cramming onto the escalators and pushing down the stairwell, spewing onto the ground floor where Yahid's men, waving their weapons menacingly, herded them out the exits.

***

Up on the third floor, Danny turned and looked towards the escalators. The hairs on the back of his neck stood up as he strained to hear above the murmur of milling customers. He looked over at Mark, who was staring his way with a knowing look. The sound of automatic fire even as faint as this had been unmistakable to men who'd lived through battle.

'Did you hear that, Scott?' Danny said.

'Er, no, hear what, old man? What's going on? You've got that funny look on your face. You know, the one that usually means trouble,' Scott said, oblivious to the shots as he smiled at a pretty blonde woman browsing the bookshelves beside them.

'Probably nothing, Scott, just stay here while I take a look,' said Danny, approaching Mark, who was up and moving his way forward, only the slightest of disjointed movements giving his prosthetic leg away.

'You heard that, right?' said Mark.

'Yep, you stay here. I'm going to run down and see what's going on.'

'No, I'm coming with you,' said Mark, his face dark and alert as his brain went into operation mode.

'You sure? If I find something, I might have to move fast,' said Danny, unintentionally letting his eyes dip to Mark's prosthetic leg.

'I can move when I have to,' said Mark, a

defiant look on his face.

'Ok. Scott, wait here. I'll be right back,' Danny said.

'Absolutely, old man, take your time,' replied Scott, still not taking much notice of Danny and Mark as he received a green light smile from the blonde and wandered in her direction.

Leaving him, they headed off towards the escalators, with Danny taking point. He watched Scott disappear with a smile at his chat up moves as he rode down to the second floor. At first glance the floor was fairly empty. A few people looked around with pale, shocked faces. A few congregated around the top of the escalators to the first floor, looking but not daring to ride them down. Stepping off the escalator, Danny and Mark moved through the kitchenware department towards the escalator to the first floor. Before they got there, the group of shoppers around its top screamed, turning in panic before running in all directions. Pulling Mark with him, Danny slid over a serving counter and landed in a crouch while Mark hit the deck arse first, the two of them surprised by the shriek of a young shop assistant hiding in the gap below the till.

'Hey, hey. Shhh, it's ok, I'm not going to hurt you,' Danny said, looking straight into her eyes and smiling to pacify her. He held his gaze for a second or so until she relaxed and nodded back to him. Turning away, Danny looked at Mark as he manoeuvred himself around to look through the counter's glass-topped display of expensive chefs' knives towards the top of the escalator. The head of Omar rose into view, followed by his body and his MP5 submachine gun. He stepped off the escalator, closely followed by two other similarly dressed and armed men.

'I am on the second floor, Yahid. I will wait for you here,' he said, listening to the response over his earpiece before looking around the floor, his face dismissive as he glanced from one insignificant shopper to another.

'Go, make sure Mark Fairbanks is not on this floor before we go up. If you find him, do not harm him. Yahid has to execute him on camera as revenge for his brother Abdullahi and a lesson to all who dare oppose us,' Omar said to the two men beside him.

Bobbing back down again, Danny looked at

Mark.

'Yahid is Abdullahi Ash-Sharm's brother,' he whispered back.

'Fuck,' Danny said before turning to the shop assistant.

'Barbra, have you got the keys to this display cabinet?' he said, reading her name badge.

'Yes, it's the small round one,' she said, pointing a shaky finger to a bunch of keys on the shelf under the till.

'Thanks,' said Danny, picking them up and unlocking the hinged glass panel at the back of the cabinet.

THREE

Sliding the expensive Japanese Aiko knife set out, Danny turned the perfectly balanced knives with incredibly sharp blades over in his hand. Spotting a leather knife holder, Danny grabbed it. He handed an eight-inch chef's knife to Mark, who tucked it inside his jacket, then slid all but one of the remaining knives into the leather slots before rolling it up and tucking it into the back of his jeans.

'Barbra, are there any stairs for the staff?' Danny said, talking calmly to the frightened woman.

'Er, yes, there's a small one through the door

over there. It goes from this floor to the third and up to the offices on the top floor. There's a larger one through the double doors next to the customer lift. That one goes all the way from the offices to the basement level,' said Barbra, pointing toward the lifts on the far side of the floor.

'Come with me, we're going up,' said Danny, barely getting the words out before the gun muzzle and the head of one of Omar's men appeared over the top of the counter.

Acting on split second impulse, Mark grabbed and pushed the MP5's muzzle to one side, while Danny reacted by thrusting the eight-inch chef's knife in his hand up under the man's chin, it's super sharp blade sliding up to the handle with surprising ease. The terrorist quivered, dying instantly as the blade entered his brain.

He dropped like a stone. His dead weight slammed the impaled knife handle lodged under his chin into the glass countertop, shattering it loudly. As shouts came from Omar on the far side of the shop floor, Mark ripped the gun out from the dead man's grip. Danny grabbed Barbra's hand and pulled her with him as they ran for the nearest stairs. Seeing Omar aiming in their direction, Danny pushed Mark through the door ahead of him while pulling Barbra past him. With an arm around each of them, Danny rugby tackled them away from the door to land in a heap at the base of the stairs to the third floor and offices. A barrage of automatic fire drummed off the wall outside before punching a row of neat round holes through the door. Leaning across Danny, Mark released a burst of fire back through the disintegrating door to deter Omar and his man from following.

'Go, go,' Danny shouted to Mark.

He didn't need telling twice and hopped up, scaling the stairs as quick as his prosthetic leg would allow him. Danny turned and took Barbra's hand once more and pulled her after Mark to the third floor. Bursting out into the book department, Mark ducked just in time to miss Scott swinging a fire extinguisher at his head.

'Whoa, steady on, Scott,' shouted Mark.

'Sorry, old boy. I heard the gunfire and thought, well I don't know what I thought, what did you find out?' said Scott, putting the extinguisher down.

'Some guy call Yahid wants to execute Mark in revenge for his brother. Are my ears still ringing or can I finally hear sirens?' Danny said, emerging from the stairs and walking straight past Scott to look out the window at a swarm of police cars and armed response units blocking off Oxford Street.

Turning back, Danny looked at the frightened faces of the twenty-or-so people huddled in the book department and then at Mark and Barbra.

'Barbra, did you say the stairs go up to the offices on the floor above us?'

'Yes,' she replied nervously.

'Ok, everyone, please follow us up to the offices. We can hold up there until the police take back the store,' Danny said, his voice calm but commanding.

'Come on, come on, we have to be quick,' said Mark as the scared shoppers moved slowly like sheep towards them.

'You ready?' said Danny, standing to one side of the door to the stairs.

'Yep,' said Mark, putting the butt of the MP5 into his shoulder and looking down the sights at the door.

Danny reached across and grabbed the door handle.

'On three. One, two, three,' he said, whipping the door open on the last count.

Mark darted in and leaned to one side as he aimed down the empty stairwell. 'It's clear,' he said, standing poised while Danny ushered people through to follow Barbra up to the office door on the floor above.

When the last person passed Danny, he tapped Mark on the shoulder. 'Here, you go up. I'll follow,' said Danny, taking the gun off Mark so he could climb the stairs easier by using the banister.

They entered the top floor offices and shut the door. Danny grabbed the end of a heavy desk and slid it loudly across the floor until it blocked the entrance.

'Chuck whatever you can find on top of that,' Danny said to Scott and Mark as he headed towards Barbra. 'Is there another way up here?'

'Er, yes, the main staff stairs next to the old goods lift, over the far side, they go all the way to the basement,' she said, pointing over everyone.

'Mark, Scott, I'm just going to check out the other stairs,' Danny shouted over the sound of filing cabinets being placed on the barricade.

FOUR

Yahid looked at the dead man slumped on the display counter. 'How did this happen?' he yelled at Omar.

'It was Fairbanks and another man. They killed him and went through that door. It leads to a narrow staircase going up,' said Omar apologetically.

'And they have his gun?'

'Yes Yahid,' Omar replied, his eyes flicking to Yahid's but lacking the courage to hold his burning gaze.

'Argh, imbeciles. Wait here, it's time to talk to the police,' Yahid said, looking around the shop floor until he saw a woman cowering behind a clothes display.

'You,' he said, marching over to her as she backed away behind the clothes in the futile attempt to make herself invisible.

She screamed as he grabbed her by the hair and hoisted her upright, pushing her ahead of him. Yahid stopped short of the mannequin display by a window facing Oxford Street. He levelled his MP5 and squeezed off a short burst. The mannequins blew apart, tumbling to the ground as the bullets passed through, shattering the front window and showering the pavement below with glass crystals. Pushing the woman forward, they stood in the glassless opening. Yahid kept tucked behind his hostage, peeping over the woman's shoulder at the police and armed response units below pointing their sniper and semi-automatic rifles up at him.

'Do not enter. We have all the doors armed with explosive devices and will execute everyone in the store if you do,' shouted Yahid, leaning the woman forward into open air to emphasise his control of the situation.

'What do you want?' came a voice through a megaphone.

'We will reveal our demands shortly,' Yahid

shouted, dragging the woman back and vanishing from sight without waiting for a reply.

Throwing the woman to the floor, he walked back towards Omar.

'Karam, status report,' Yahid said over the radio.

'We're through the first lock on schedule,' Karam said above a screechy drilling noise.

'Good. Nasr, status report.'

'The door is open, we're cutting through the brickwork now,' came a crackly response from Nasr.

'Ok, let me know when you are through,' said Yahid turning his attention back to Omar. 'We continue as planned. We find Fairbanks and execute him live on social media for the world to see. Then we blow the place before they drop a team on the roof to storm the building.'

'Yes Yahid,' said Omar, waving the men over.

'Shan, Yanni, this is Yahid. We are going up to three.'

'This is Shan. We are heading up the main staircase now.'

'This is Yanni, I'm heading up the staff stairs.'

Full of confidence at this planning, Yahid

followed behind Omar and two men as they stepped onto the escalator and moved smoothly upwards, their eyes darting left and right as they searched the approaching floor. With their guns up and ready, the knowledge that Fairbanks and a stranger had one of their weapons adding to the tension.

Stepping off, the empty book department lay ahead of them. They stepped to one side and spun around, scanning the toy department behind them. A noise over on the far side caused them to spin around and point their guns. They relaxed a little as Shan and his two men appeared from the main staircase.

Yahid walked into the book department. He moved up to the signing desk with Mark Fairbanks' books piled on top. Picking one up, Yahid turned to face the others. Dropping it, he flew into a rage, grabbing the edge of the table and flipping it over as he shouted. 'Where is he?'

A noise behind a floor-to-ceiling bookcase display caught his attention. His head whipped in its direction like an animal hunting its prey. Letting his rifle drop on its shoulder strap, he drew his handgun and moved silently towards it.

When he reached the end, he spun around it to face an old couple huddled behind. The old man didn't flinch as his wife cowered behind him. He stared Yahid defiantly in the eye, a signed copy of Mark Fairbanks' book still clutched in his hand.

'Where did Fairbanks go, old man?' said Yahid, just about in control of his anger.

'You think I'd tell you, boy? You're worth less than the shit on my shoe,' the old man said.

'You might want to rethink your answer, old man,' Yahid said, moving the gun across to point at his wife's head.

'Tell him, Frank,' his terrified wife said.

The conflict was clear to see on the ex-serviceman's face, a lifetime of not giving in being compromised by his love for his wife. Seconds passed as the tension grew until he finally gave in.

'They went through there. Now fuck off and leave us in peace,' he said, turning his back on Yahid to comfort his wife.

Yahid's face contorted with rage. 'You don't tell me to fuck off,' he yelled, placing the end of his gun on the back of the old man's head and pulling the trigger.

The noise made everyone jump. As the old man slumped to the floor, his wife stood rigid in shock, her face and clothes covered in her husband's blood and brain matter. As she opened her mouth to say something, Yahid centred the gun on her, shooting her in the head and dropping her to the floor next to her husband.

'They went through there,' Yahid said, his face composed, the anger in check once more.

FIVE

Moving across the office to the staff stairs, Danny noticed a pale-faced office clerk talking nervously on one of the office phones.

'Hey, are you talking to the police?' Danny said, his voice calm and body language authoritative.

'Er, yes,' the clerk stammered.

'Give it here,' Danny said.

The clerk handed the phone over without a murmur.

'Hello, stay on the line, Neville, hello.'

'Hello, this is Daniel Pearson. You can verify who I am with the Chief of the Secret Intelligence Service, Edward Jenkins. Now listen up, the store has been taken over by a terrorist known as Yahid Ash-Sharm and at least ten men. They are all armed with MP5 submachine guns and various other weapons.'

'Ok, what do they want?' came the voice on the other end.

'Yahid wants to execute ex-SAS Captain Mark Fairbanks for killing his terrorist brother Abdullahi Ash-Sharm while on active duty. We've disarmed one terrorist and barricaded ourselves in the offices on the top floor,' Danny said, staring nervously at the top of the staff stairs.

'Right, Mr Pearson, how many people are with you?'

'Eh, around thirty. Hello, hello? They've cut the lines,' Danny said, handing the phone back to Neville before heading for the stairs.

Pulling the fire door open, Danny paused for a few seconds when it creaked loudly at the halfway point. When no one came, he slid through, placing his hand on the back of the door to soften its closing. Edging towards the banister, Danny took a darting look down the stairwell. When no guns pointed up at him, he moved forward for a proper look. Five storeys down, he could hear a loud grinding noise, and plumes of brick dust hovered in the air around the base of the stairs. While trying to make out what was going on, he spotted a hand appear on a banister below. Shadows moved from the second floor as they made their way up to the third. Seeing a shoulder, Danny lent back out of view just before Yanni's head turned and looked up towards the top floor. He stood motionless, watching for a while before turning back and following his men out the doors to the third floor. Danny took another look down, then turned to go back into the offices. He paused for a second to study the ancient freight elevator beside him, then went back inside, moving over to Mark and Scott, deep in thought.

'Why here?' he said to Mark.

'What do you mean, why here?' Mark replied, puzzled.

'There's something not right about this. How hard would it have been to find out where you live?' Danny said to Mark.

'Er, not very, I suppose, social media, Facebook posts or my literary agent.'

'So why take over an entire store to get one

man? You have no way out and you know the police will storm the building sooner or later,' said Danny, frowning.

'Because they're a bunch of crazy fanatics,' said Scott, chipping in.

'No, I don't buy it. They're grinding or drilling in the basement for something. Hang on,' said Danny, looking around. 'Barbra, hey, over here.'

Barbra walked over, managing a smile despite her nerves.

'What's at the bottom of the staff stairs?' Danny asked.

'The basement,' she said, confused.

'No, sorry, that's not what I meant. What's lies at the base of the stairs?'

'Er nothing, the original goods lift. It doesn't work. It was condemned years ago. Eh, the doors to the basement level shop floor, next to the jewellery counter. Oh, and the old air raid tunnel to the subway, but that's been bricked up since the end of the Second World War.'

'That's it. They're going to get away through the subway tunnels,' said Danny.

'I say, chaps, you don't suppose they are here

to steal that 35-million-pound necklace thing on display? What's it called, *La* something?' said Scott.

'*La Perfection Mouawad* diamond necklace, but that's not all. The jewellery department has several million pounds' worth of jewellery in the displays and in the strong room,' said Barbra.

'I reckon you're right, Scott. Yahid plans to take over the store and kill Mark in revenge and a diversion while they escape through the Underground tunnels with all the jewellery,' said Danny, looking back towards the staff stairs. 'I need a closer look.'

'Then I'm coming with you,' said Mark, a determined look on his face.

'Outstanding. Off you trot. I'll stay here and keep an eye on things,' said Scott, patting them on the back.

'Oh no you don't. Follow me, Scotty boy, I need you to do something for me,' said Danny, smiling as he moved to the staff stairs.

'Hmm, ok. But if you get me killed, I'm coming back to haunt you,' said Scott, following reluctantly.

As before, Danny eased the door open to the

stairwell, holding it at the creak for Mark and Scott to pass through before easing it silently shut behind him.

'Clear,' whispered Mark after a darting look.

The three of them leaned forward and looked down towards the basement. The grinding had stopped to be replaced by the dull thuds of a lump hammer on bricks.

'Right, Scott, take this,' said Danny, handing him the MP5 submachine gun. 'It's on single shot, ok? Now listen, Yahid's men are on the floor below. It won't be long before they decide to come up here. As soon as you see the door to the third floor open, gently squeeze off a couple of rounds. It'll force them back and buy us some time,' said Danny, tucking the butt of the rifle into Scott's shoulder and pointing him in the right direction.

'Ok, but I'm not sure I could shoot anybody in cold blood.'

'That's ok, Scott, I'm not asking you to, just keep them from coming up here,' Danny said, pulling out the leather roll with knives in from the back of his jeans.

Pulling out a flexible fish knife, he slid it

between the concertina lift door and frame. He worked it up until he felt the door latch, then after a bit of twisting, popped the locking latch up and pulled the rusted door open with a painful screech. The three of them froze and all looked at each other, only relaxing when the echo of hammering continued from the basement. Looking down the lift shaft, Danny could see each floor lit by a dull bulkhead fixed to the wall. He followed the steel cable down to see the lift carriage sitting down on the basement level.

'You ready for this?' Danny said to Mark while taking his jacket off.

'Try stopping me,' Mark said with a grin.

'We'll slide down to the carriage and pop the door to the basement floor,' said Danny, wrapping his jacket around the steel cables as he grabbed them and slid down out of sight. Mark did the same, leaving Scott alone, awkwardly pointing the rifle at the third-floor door.

'Why couldn't we have just gone straight to the pub?' Scott muttered to himself.

SIX

To one side of the book department, Omar pulled the door to the stairs open. His two men charged in, one pointed his gun down and the other pointed up the stairs towards the office's door.

'There is no one here, Yahid,' Omar said, looking in after his men.

Yahid marched into the stairwell. He looked down at the debris on the stairs and light coming through the damaged door to the second floor. Stepping across, he looked up at the office door. Shadows and blurry images of piled up furniture and filing cabinets filled the frosted glass panel in its centre.

'They are up there,' Yahid said, tapping his radio. 'Shan, join Yanni and go up the staff stairs. Fairbanks is on the top floor. Kill who you like, but I need Fairbanks alive for the execution film.'

'Yes Yahid,' came Shan's reply.

'Go up and break the door down,' Yahid ordered Omar's men.

They started up the stairs, freezing when shots sounded, and someone screamed over the earpiece.

'Yanni, Shan, what's happening?'

'Someone fired at us from the top of the stairs, Yanni has been hit in the leg.'

'I see him,' came Nasr's voice, followed by a hail of fire echoing up the stairs from the basement.

'Did you get him?' shouted Yahid over the racket.

'I don't think—argh.'

'Nasr, Nasr,' yelled Yahid.

***

After following Danny's instructions and

popping off a couple of shots the second the doors to the third floor opened, Scott glanced down just in time to see Nasr aiming up at him with his MP5.

'Oh God, oh God, oh God,' muttered Scott, dropping to the floor as bullets raced up the stairwell and ricocheted off the concrete ceiling at the top, whizzing and thudding into the floor and walls around him.

'Please don't let me be hit, please don't let me be hit.' said Scott, patting himself down with a sigh of relief at the lack of any blood.

Inside the lift shaft, Danny and Mark lifted the escape hatch on top of the old freight elevator and dropped inside. When the firing started, Danny drew an eight-inch carving knife out of the leather roll while Mark grabbed the handle of the loading doors. Tensing up, Danny nodded, and Mark pulled the doors open as fast as he could. Nasr only had a split second to turn his head before Danny thrust the knife up under his ribcage, twisting it to rip the arteries from his heart before lowering Nasr's twitching body to the ground. Dropping the knife, Danny picked up Nasr's sub-machine gun and spun around at the sound of footsteps charging up a small rubble covered staircase behind an open cast iron door. At the first sight of a face and gun barrel, Danny fired off a shot, striking the man in the head, blowing the man back off his feet.

'Nice shot,' said Mark, heading for the downed man and taking his MP5 off him.

'Nah, I was aiming for his heart,' Danny joked. 'Scott, you alright, buddy?' Danny yelled up the stairwell.

'I'm never going anywhere with you again,' came Scott's protest from above.

'Yeah, he's alright,' Danny said, taking spare ammunition magazines out of Nasr's vest and passing one to Mark.

They moved either side of the doors to the basement shop floor. Danny reached round and gently pushed the door open a crack with the barrel of his gun. He recoiled sharply as bullets ripped through the wood.

'They'll probably have men on the ground floor by the entrance doors as well. What do you reckon, first floor and work up?' Danny whispered across to Mark.

'Yeah, we'll go after Yahid. He won't expect

us to attack from below.'

The two men backed away. Danny let Mark go up first, covering the rear for Mark as he used the banister to steady himself on the climb up to the first floor.

They approached the doors the same way as before. When no fire came, they slid through, moving low amongst the menswear displays for cover. Heading for the escalators, Mark's prosthetic leg slid out on the tiled floor, sending him down on his knee.

'You alright?' Danny said, covering the floor ahead with the rifle while Mark regained balance.

'Yeah, I'm fine. The leg's pretty good, but there's no substitute for the real thing.'

SEVEN

'What's happening?' yelled Yahid, leaving Omar and his men to break into the office.

'This is Karam. Nasr and Akeam are dead and whoever did it has their weapons.'

'Where did they go?' ordered Yahid, marching over to Shan as he tried to stem the bleeding from Yanni's leg.

'Up the back stairs, I heard someone on the top floor. I think they went back into the offices.'

'Alright, have you got into the vault yet?' Yahid said, the gun trembling in his hand as he tried to keep his anger in check.

'Another ten minutes, we're on the last lock now.'

'Good, let me know when you're in,' Yahid

said, looking down at Yanni on the floor. 'Let me see.'

Shan moved a jumper he'd grabbed off a clothes rail to stem the bleeding. As soon as the pressure was off, blood started pumping profusely out of the wound.

'We can't carry him. He is of no use to us now,' said Yahid, his face without emotion. Moving the gun up to Yanni's head, Yahid pulled the trigger. Still holding the bloodied jumper, Shan stared up at Yahid, a questioning look on his face. Yahid moved his gun across to Shan. 'You have a problem with that?' he said.

'No, no, Yahid, of course not.'

'Good, get up to the offices and call me when you have Fairbanks. Go, make it quick, it is only a matter of time before the police try to enter the building and we need to be long gone by then.'

***

Apart from a few customers cowering behind shop displays, the first floor was clear of Yahid's men.

'Ready for the second floor?' Danny said, stepping onto the escalator, his rifle up in front of him as he scanned for terrorists.

'Right with you, brother.'

'Just like old times,' said Danny.

'Yeah, with less dirt and heat.'

'At the top, I'll take right, you take left.'

'Roger that,' said Mark, his back to Danny's, covering the far side of the shop floor as it came into view.

***

'Daniel, where the hell are you?' muttered Scott, peeping over the banister at the empty stairwell below him. He winced at the sight of Nasr's body lying in a pool of blood at the bottom of the stairs. The sound of shouts and screams from the office behind him made him jump out of his skin.

'Oh no, what now?' he said, tentatively pulling the office door open and poking his head around.

People were hurrying away from the barricaded door as bullets punched through the glass, embedding themselves into the wooden desks and filing cabinets that blocked the way in.

'Come on, Daniel, I need you,' said Scott, moving back to the stairs to see if he and Mark were in sight.

As he leaned over, Shan and his men pointed their guns up at him from the third-floor landing. Scott's eyes went wide. He dived backwards, crashing through the office door a split second before a stream of bullets ripped around behind him, gouging and splintering the wooden banisters and door frame. Glass crystals rained down on Scott as the window blew in from the door. Staff and customers shrieked and screamed at the noise. Panicking, Scott accidentally knocked the MP5 sub-machine gun into automatic, shocking himself and the people around him when he unleashed a rapid stream of white-hot bullets ricocheting around the staircase. Taking his finger off the trigger, Scott stayed sitting on the office floor, shaking and breathing heavily.

***

Stepping off the escalator onto the second floor, Danny whipped his head towards the staff stairs and sound of gunfire echoing from above. He started to move when shots from behind him made him jump and spin around. Two terrorists dropped to the floor amongst the kitchenware as Mark stepped off the escalator, smoke still rising from the barrel of his gun.

'Either of them Yahid?'

'No, I don't think so,' said Mark.

'Let's go up again. I've gotta make sure Scott's ok,' said Danny, heading for the escalator to the third floor.

Covering each other's backs, Danny and Mark rode up to the book department. They stepped off halfway between the sound of gunfire from the small staircase to the office and gunfire from the staff stairwell on the far side of the shop floor. Danny paused momentarily, looking from the book department to the staff stairs.

'Come on, we'll help your friend Scott first,' said Mark, knowing what Danny was thinking.

'Sounds like a shitstorm whichever way we go,' said Danny, covering the rear as he followed Mark.

Peeling apart, Danny and Mark placed their backs on the wall on either side of the heavy fire doors to the stairwell. With an unspoken synchronicity, they both leaned across and peeped through the small windows in the doors. Shan and his two men were sliding along the wall, making their way up the stairs to the offices.

'Why don't you bloody people just sod off?' came Scott's frustrated shout, followed by a hail of uncontrolled automatic fire.

Just before Scott's gun clicked empty, two bullets punched through the fire door inches away from Danny's head. Mark glanced at him, grinning. 'Don't look at me, he's your mate,' he said, cocking his head towards the door for them to go in.

'Don't I know it. On three. One, two, three,' Danny said, bursting through the door, catching Shan and his men in his sights as they moved on Scott's firing position.

Danny tapped two bullets into Shan while Mark dropped the other two as they turned at the sound of the doors opening. When the noise of gunfire finished echoing around the stairwell,

Danny looked up at the top floor. 'Any of them Yahid?' he said to Mark.

'Unfortunately not,' Mark said, turning the men over.

'You ok, Scotty boy?' Danny yelled up.

Scott's shocked face appeared peeping through the banisters. 'No, I'm bloody well not,' he said, his floppy brown hair standing on end and his clothes all dishevelled. 'Oh my gosh, did I do that?' Scott said, looking at the dead men.

'No Scott, you didn't, but you did nearly shoot me in the head,' Danny said, moving past the dead men on his way up.

'Mmm, yes well, eh, probably the best place to shoot you, considering the lack of anything in there.'

'Thanks, Scott, I love you too.'

EIGHT

Stepping off the main stairs onto the ground floor, Yahid paused at all the distant sound of gunfire. 'Omar, are you in yet? Have you got Fairbanks?'

'Not yet, but we are nearly through to the office.'

'Shan, where are you? Shan, SHAN!' Yahid shouted, his face contorting in anger and frustration. He moved towards the main doors, still chained shut with explosive devices taped to the handles.

'What's going on out there?' he asked his man tucked to one side of them.

'They're definitely planning something. Looks

like the special ops teams have arrived.'

'Ok, keep an eye on them. I'm going down to the vault. Ten minutes, we pull out,' Yahid said, patting his man on the back and heading off down the escalator to the basement. As he approached the jewellery department, Karam burst out from the vault room with his sub-machine gun pointing in Yahid's direction.

'It's ok, it's me. Are you in yet?' said Yahid, a hint of panic in his voice.

'Yes, come see,' said Karam.

Following Karam inside, Yahid set eyes on the old vault. Built at the same time as the store to hold expensive jewellery stock, cash takings, and staff wages in the age when cash was king, the twelve-by-twelve-foot steel-lined room now held bespoke watches and jewellery worth hundreds of thousands each and the *La Perfection Mouawad* necklace. Its solid steel door was wide open, an industrial drill still held fast over its destroyed locks by a powerful magnetic jig. White-hot metal filings sparked across the floor as Yahid's safe cracker ground through the last lock on an internal gate, the diamond-tipped cutting blade moving through the metal like a knife through butter until the deadbolt fell in two and the gate swung open, leaving the *La Perfection Mouawad* necklace in full view inside its glass display case.

'Bag it up, we leave in five minutes,' said Yahid, turning to leave the room.

'But what about Fairbanks?' Karam called after him.

Yahid turned and glared at him angrily. 'Just bag it up and be ready to leave,' he said before walking out the door. He turned and went through the doors to the staff stairwell, frowning at Nasr and the dead man lying on the steps of the tunnel to the Underground. 'Omar, have you got Fairbanks?'

***

'We are going in now,' said Omar as the two men in front of him broke the remains of the office door in two and pushed the filing cabinet on the other side away from the entrance. Moving forward to enter, the man in front flew backwards as if snapped back by a bungee cord, tumbling past Omar into a crumpled heap at the bottom of the stairs. Before Omar could comprehend what was happening, Mark's face looking down the sights of his MP5 appeared in the doorway as he fired off another round at the other man's head, the bullet taking the back of his head away and showering Omar in blood and brain matter.

'Oh God, he is here, Yahid. Fairbanks has killed them all. We have lost,' Omar said, turning in a panic and running for the bottom of the stairs. As he burst out into the book department, Danny cracked him in the side of the head with the butt of his sub-machine gun. Omar went down like a felled tree, his radio and earpiece rattling across the floor with his gun as his face slapped onto the tiled floor.

Mark and Scott joined Danny as he checked Omar was out and didn't have any other weapons.

'Yahid?' Danny said, turning to Mark.

'Damn. No, that's not him,' Mark said, frustrated that the man had still eluded them.

'Where the hell is he?' Danny said, picking up the radio and earpiece from the floor.

'Omar, Omar, get to the basement. We're going to blow the ground floor and go, come

NOW,' crackled out of the little speaker in Danny's ear.

'He's going for the tunnel,' Danny said, picking up the MP5 and taking off at a full sprint.

'Danny, wait up,' shouted Mark, running after him as fast as his prosthetic leg would allow him, which was not fast enough to catch Danny.

Seeing him disappear down the main stairs, Mark hurtled recklessly after him, losing his footing and falling several steps before picking himself up and continuing down.

'Well, I suppose it's my job to watch you then,' Scott said, kicking Omar in the leg to make sure he was still out.

The loud whomp of a helicopter over the building made Scott look up the stairs to the office. Within seconds he could hear breaking glass followed by screams, followed by shouts of, *'Get down!'*.

Omar's hand grabbing his ankle made Scott shriek. Reacting in blind panic, Scott smashed the butt of his gun onto the bridge of Omar's nose, breaking it and knocking him back out.

'Oh, eh, sorry, old man, but you really

shouldn't go grabbing people.'

'You, drop the weapon, down on the ground. Now,' came a shout as a special ops team swept down from the offices.

'Steady on, gentlemen. I'm one of the good guys,' said Scott, dropping the weapon as if it were on fire.

'Get on your front, hands behind your head,' the guy shouted before talking into his throat mic. 'Delta team in, we have five hostiles down and one injured. There is no sign of Daniel Pearson or Mark Fairbanks or Yahid Ash-Sharm. Over.'

'I say, excuse me, large dangerous looking man,' interrupted Scott.

'Shut up and stay down,' yelled the man, his eyes sharp and focused through his balaclava.

'Alright, Mr Smartypants, but I just thought you might like to know they're headed to the basement to stop this Yahid fellow escaping with millions of pounds worth of jewellery through some old tunnel leading into the Underground network,' said Scott with a smug smile.

While one guy zip-tied Omar's hands and feet, and another one moved over to Scott, the team leader stared at Scott, ticking through options. 'Not him,' he said to the man about to tie Scott's hands. 'All teams to the basement. Yahid Ash-Sharm is attempting to escape into the Underground network. Pearson and Fairbanks are in pursuit.'

In the blink of an eye, the team headed off, splitting in two as half went down the escalator and the other half down the stairs.

NINE

Danny jumped down half the stairs to the ground floor. He turned, sliding a little as prepared to launch himself down towards the basement level. At the same time, the doors to the store disappeared in a bright flash, followed a millisecond later by an earth-shattering boom, followed by a blast wave that punched Danny in the back and propelled him down the stairs.

'Fuck,' Danny yelled from a painful landing where the stairs turned. He shook his head, disorientated, and snapped his gun up at the sound of clattering footsteps above him.

'Whoa, it's me,' shouted Mark, half sliding down the banister, half bouncing on his good leg to get down as fast as he could. 'You ok?'

'Yeah, nothing broken,' Danny said, cracking his neck to one side.

'Good, now are you going to stand there like a tart all day or are we going to catch Yahid?' Mark said, grinning as he moved past Danny towards the basement.

'Yes sir,' Danny said, following him.

***

'Is that all of you?' Yahid said to the two men from the ground floor.

'Yes Yahid, we waited but none of the others came.'

Yahid looked at the three black canvas bags on the jewellery department counter and Karam and the safe cracker. Without warning he brought his MP5 up and pulled the trigger, emptying the rest of the magazine into the two men before throwing the empty gun on the floor. Clearly in on the plan, Karam raised his gun at the safe cracker.

'No, no, take it, take it all. I won't say anything to the police, please,' he stammered, his eyes wide in panic, his mind desperately trying to work out a way to save himself.

Karam just pulled the trigger, turned away and grabbing two of the canvas bags before the man hit the floor. Yahid zipped the last bag up over the *La Perfection Mouawad* diamond necklace and swung it up onto his shoulder. Turning, the two men pushed their way through the fire doors to the staff stairwell and turned down the dimly lit steps and headed down. Halfway down the narrow tunnel, Yahid stopped and pulled out a block of C4 plastic explosive with a small timer attached.

'Here, set it to one minute, Karam.'

***

Hearing the gunshots, Danny and Mark flattened themselves against the wall and took a cautious look into the basement shop floor. Two men fell to the floor before Karam shot the safe cracker and followed Yahid out the doors to the staff stairs.

'The short one is Yahid,' said Mark to Danny.

'Let's move,' Danny said, taking off at a full sprint.

By the time Mark caught him up, Danny had peeped through the small window in the door and was pushing his way through the door.

'Shh, do you hear that?' Danny said at the entrance to the tunnel.

'Yeah, footsteps, not too far ahead by the sounds of it,' said Mark.

'I'll go ahead and wait for you at the bottom of the steps,' said Danny, knowing Mark needed more time to get down and wouldn't be able to shoot and steady himself as he descended.

'Ok, go, go.'

Danny gave him a nod and went off as fast as he could in the dim light from the decades-old bulkheads fixed to the tunnel wall. He'd got twenty or so meters ahead of Mark, when a faint red glow on the tunnel wall beside him caught his eye. Glancing in its direction, Danny recoiled at the sight of a timer on a lump of plastic explosive, its clock ticking down to six seconds.

'Mark, get back,' Danny yelled, dropping his gun.

Deciding he could get away faster by hurtling down the stairs rather than trying to get back up, Danny leapt down great chunks of steps, slipping on the final few and tumbling out onto a flat surface as the devices went off. The sound was ear shattering in the confined space. A cloud of dust and rubble showered him as he lay on the floor.

***

Coughing and blinded by dust, Mark tried to pull himself back up the stairs. When he didn't move, he realised his prosthetic leg was buried in the rubble from the blocked tunnel. Feeling behind him, Mark felt for the kitchen knife Danny had given him. Pulling it out, he cut his trouser leg off at the knee, pulled himself out of the leg socket, he proceeded to hop back up the stairs. When he got to the top, half a dozen bright LED lights blinded him.

'Freeze! Get down on the floor NOW!' came multiple shouts.

'Stand down, it's Fairbanks,' came a voice from the back.

The unit parted, and a suited man came to the front.

'Edward Jenkins, MI6. Are you ok, Mr Fairbanks? Where's Yahid?' he said, looking over Mark at the blocked tunnel.

'He's in the Underground; Danny's gone after him.'

'Ok. Control, this is Jenkins. Get a medic for Mr Fairbanks and get onto London Underground. I want CCTV access and maps of all tunnels, used and abandoned, and I want it now. Yahid Ash-Sharm is in there somewhere and I want to know where he's headed.'

TEN

When the dust had cleared, Danny looked around him. He'd come out on an old, abandoned platform, decades of grey dust covering the once shiny tracks. A line of strip lights still lit up the empty platform. Snapping back to his hunt for Yahid, Danny looked left. The redundant train tunnel was boarded off. He turned right, the far end looked the same. Shaking the dust out of his unruly mop of hair, Danny headed for the cutout in the side of the platform tunnel that would have served as the entrance and exit. Hearing his footsteps echo loudly, amplified by the circular shape of the tunnel, Danny moved into the exit and stood still, listening.

There they are. Faint footsteps off to the left.

Danny set off, his view ahead impaired by less lighting, and the tunnel's curve off to the right. Thirty metres up, he came across an open metal door in the tunnel wall, its lock freshly forced open. Entering the gloom, Danny could see light twenty metres ahead. An identical metal door with its lock forced greeted him at the other end. Stepping out, he realised it was an access tunnel between the old, abandoned line and the very much alive Central underground line. A gust of air made him pull back, just before the Tube train pushing it through the tunnel, shot past in a blur of carriages and unaware passengers. Danny followed it with his eyes as it clattered away, stopping at a light in the distance. Thinking about where the store was on Oxford

Street, Danny guessed the light must be a platform at Oxford Circus.

On the other side of the tracks, barely visible in the dark, Danny spotted Yahid and Karam heading in its direction. Crossing over, Danny jumped well clear of the live rails and their 630 volts. Conscious that he could lose them at the busy station, Danny ran at full pelt, closing the gap quickly as Karam and Yahid struggled with their heavy bags of stolen jewellery. Swinging his arm around Karam's neck, Danny pulled him back, tightening his grip into a choke hold. Karam dropped the bags and felt for his handgun. Grabbing Karam's wrist with his free hand, Danny pulled ever tighter on his neck. The wind in the tunnel started to build as Danny watched Yahid stop and start to turn up ahead.

Shit.

With a light growing brighter behind him, Danny released Karam and dropped back into an alcove on the side of the tunnel wall. Pulling his gun, Karam spun around. He froze like a rabbit caught in headlights as the underground train lit up his face.

The front corner hit him with a sickening thud, the impact shattering bones and organs before sending him flying into the tunnel wall. He flopped lifelessly to the ground as the train's emergency brakes locked on, its wheels screeching on the rails before it shuddered to a stop.

Danny felt something hard push at the base of his spine. Reaching behind him, he pulled the leather knife roll out. Getting to his feet, he leaned forward and looked between the train and the tunnel wall. He tucked back in double quick as Yahid fired wildly in his direction. When the firing stopped, Danny took a quick second look. Yahid was running for the station platform. Pushing off the wall, Danny leaped over Karam and powered after him. Yahid swung the bag onto the platform and climbed up after it. He threw it back on his shoulder and moved further up the platform, pushing through panicked passengers as they ran, hid or froze at the sight of his gun. Moving for the exit, Yahid turned and aimed back at Danny, firing his last few shots. His turn had been too slow and his aim too erratic. Danny saw it coming and dived below the end of the platform, only rising and hopping up onto the platform when he heard the gun click empty.

'Give it up, Yahid, there's nowhere to go,' Danny said, moving slowly forwards with one hand behind his back.

With a look of hatred on his face, Yahid backed away, his hand moving behind his tactical vest to pull out a six-inch hunting knife. In a flash he darted across and grabbed a pregnant woman by the hair as she cowered by the platform seating. Moving her close, he put his arm around her, resting the knife on the side of her throat.

'Let the woman go, Yahid,' Danny said, his eyes narrowing, hawk-like, with unwavering focus.

Yahid didn't answer. He maintained hateful eye contact while backing away towards the exit.

'Don't worry, I'm not going to let him hurt you,' Danny said calmly, taking a step forward for every one Yahid took back.

As he backed in front of the exit tunnel, a group of office workers bumped Yahid from behind as they jostled onto the platform, eager to catch the next train. Yahid shifted to one side, turning his head in panic, the central line of his body momentarily visible from behind his pregnant hostage.

The moment was all Danny needed.

Raising the incredibly sharp and perfectly balanced six-inch Japanese Aiko knife in the air, Danny flicked his arm forward, throwing the knife at Yahid. It struck just above the breastbone, in the soft flesh of the throat, slicing through his windpipe until it lodged in the vertebrae at the back of his neck. Yahid released the woman, dropping his knife and canvas bag as he scrambled for the handle of the impaled knife. Gripping it with shaky hands, Yahid pulled it out. A heavy flow of blood poured from the wound the second it was out. Coughing and spluttering to clear the blood pouring down his severed windpipe, Yahid clutched at his throat and staggered towards the platform edge. He turned and stared at Danny with narrow hateful eyes. His mouth opened and closed as he tried to speak, but only bloody bubbles came out. Drowning in his own blood, Yahid fell straight back, disappearing off the platform on to the tracks. Walking forward, Danny watched Yahid's body twitch and jerk on the live rail before lying still, smoke and the smell of burning flesh filling the air.

'Everyone down on the floor now!' came a shout from behind him.

Covered in black grime and exhausted, Danny turned to face the special ops unit. 'Really?' he said sarcastically.

The team parted, and the familiar, suited figure of Edward Jenkins walked through.

'You ok?' Edward said, looking over the platform edge at Yahid.

'Yeah, there's another one down the tunnel,' Danny said, pointing towards the stopped train.

'And the diamond necklace?'

'In the bag. Are Scott and Mark ok?' Danny said.

'Yes, they're fine. I'll take you to them,' Edward said, leading Danny out.

ELEVEN

They exited Oxford Circus tube station and walked towards the cordoned-off Harrington's department store. Edward used his ID and was shown through and pointed in the direction of a row of ambulances, treating the shoppers and staff for minor injuries and shock. He spotted Mark sitting on the back of one. A police officer had managed to dig his leg out for him and he'd just put it back on. He gave a grin when he saw Danny and hopped down.

'You'll be walking in circles on that thing,' Danny chuckled, looking at the bent inwards foot on Mark's prosthetic leg.

'Nothing's going to stop me walking away from this fucking place,' Mark joked back.

'You and me both, mate. Where's Scott?'

'Next ambulance along, and Danny?'

'Yeah.'

'Thank you for being there, brother,' Mark said with a look brothers-in-arms knew well.

Danny just gave him a knowing smile and a nod, then headed off to find Scott. It didn't take long. He heard Scott before he saw him.

'Yes, my dear, that's when I fought off four of the terrorists single-handed. If you'd care to have dinner sometime, I'll tell you all about it,' said Scott to an attractive paramedic.

'I'd take him up on that. He's a proper hero, this one,' said Danny, poking his head around the door of the ambulance.

'Er, yes, well. Daniel, how good of you not to be dead. You do look a frightful state though.'

'Thanks for the concern. You ok, mate?' Danny said, genuinely worried about his best friend.

'I'm fine, old boy, but I'm never going anywhere with you again.'

'Oh really? That's a shame. I was going to get cleaned up and continue our original plans for the Dog and Duck,' Danny said, turning to walk away.

'Well, hang on, let's not be too hasty. I'll come, but you're paying,' said Scott, breaking into a wide grin.

'Hey, you're the rich one, why am I paying?'

'That's why I'm rich, old boy, now lead the way.'

Please, please, please leave a review for
A Short Time To Kill

As an self published indie author, I can't stress enough how important your Amazon reviews are to getting my work out there.

I love writing these books for you, it takes eight months of hard work to create each one. So please take a few minutes to click the book link below, scroll down to reviews and leave a short review or just star rate it.

Thank you so much
Stephen Taylor

Review A Short Time To Kill

Choose your next Danny Pearson novel

The Danny Pearson books can be read in any order,
But here they are in the order they were written:

Vodka Over London Ice

The London mob clash with the Russian Mafia.
The death and violence escalate, putting Danny's family in
danger. Danny Pearson has to end the war, before more
family die…

Execution of Faith

Terrorists and mercenary killers plot to change the balance of
world power. Can Danny Pearson stop them or will this be
his downfall…

Who Holds The Power

As a Secret organisation kills, corrupts, and influences its way
to global domination. Danny Pearson must stop them and
their deadly Chinese assassin in his most dangerous adventure
to date…

Alive Until I Die

When government cutbacks threaten project Dragonfly.
General Rufus McManus takes direct action to secure its
future. Deep undercover with his life on the line, can Danny
survive long enough to bring him to justice…

Sport of Kings

When Danny's old SAS buddy goes missing, Danny's unit
reunite to find him. When they follow Smudge's trail, they

find themselves on the wrong side of an international drug smuggling operation and the sport of kings, an exclusive hunt of a deadly nature...

Blood Runs Deep

Five Years Ago (Vodka Over London Ice) The London mob clashed with the Russian Mafia. Death and violence escalated, putting Danny's family in danger. Danny Pearson ended the war, or so he thought…

Command to Kill

When Australian billionaire Theodore Blazer takes advantage of todays plugged in world with sinister intentions, Danny has to travel to the far side of the earth to save his friend Scott and stop the world falling apart…

<u>Danny Pearson Shorts</u>
SNIPE
Heavy Traffic
The Timekeepers Box
The Book Signing

Amazon Author Page

Available on Amazon

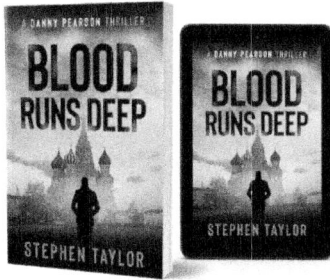

Read on for an extract from
Blood Runs Deep

ONE

Looking at his watch, then up at the grand, mid-19th century I of the Gare du Nord Paris Metro, Danny Pearson continued to look for his target while polishing off the rest of his Whopper burger. He glanced at the man's picture on his phone, then sat back under Burger King's outside canopy, and resumed his watchful eye.

Five minutes later, his target, Miles Marshbrook, emerged from the train station. The tall, skinny, nervous man with a leather overnight bag slung across his shoulder looked both ways before scurrying across the road. He walked past Danny and disappeared out of sight, heading off down the Boulevard de Strasbourg.

Danny drained the rest of his drink through

the straw. He was in no hurry to follow; he knew where Marshbrook was heading. What did interest him were the two Middle Eastern men who exited the train station a minute later. They took a quick glance either way before crossing the road, their eyes locking back onto Marshbrook as they followed him down the Boulevard de Strasbourg.

Danny slid the food wrappers into the bin and strolled out of the canopied shade into the hot summer sun. With the boulevard full of Parisians and tourists, Danny knew Marshbrook would be relatively safe until he checked into his reservation at the Hotel Relais Du Louvre, opposite the famous Louvre art museum next to the river Seine. His brief from Howard was simple: meet Miles Marshbrook in room 18 of the hotel, and exchange money for the information Mr Marshbrook claims to have regarding the identity of an inside man who has been selling Ministry of Defence weapons designs to the Middle East.

Not wanting to turn up late to the party, and due to the location of the meet, Danny had taken an educated guess that Marshbrook would take the train into the city. Following at the rear of the procession, Danny studied the look and movement of the two Middle Eastern men ahead of him. They were wearing zipped-up jackets even though it was swelteringly hot, suggesting concealed weapons, and they walked with purpose: upright, regimented, military trained with rock-steady, focused heads on solid necks. Danny's best guess was Saudi secret services.

They crossed onto Boulevard de Sebastopol and continued down towards the river, the two men ahead peeling off and entering a shop while Marshbrook walked into Starbucks to get a coffee. Danny continued to walk along the tree-lined boulevard, passing all three of them to cross the road and turn down towards the Pont au Change bridge. Picking up his pace, he followed the river towards the Louvre. Within five minutes, Danny was sitting on a bench across from a grand Gothic church, and in sight of the entrance to the Hotel Relais Du Louvre.

It didn't take long for Marshbrook to approach the hotel from the more direct route. He looked around nervously before entering, obvious to the trained eye that he didn't know what he was supposed to be looking for. The two Middle Eastern men entered the hotel a minute later, still visible to Danny through the front window as they pretended to look at the tourist board inside the foyer while Marshbrook checked in. Moving closer, Danny tucked in behind an Enterprise rental van parked opposite the hotel. Peeping around the back of it, he could see Marshbrook taking the room keys from the receptionist and heading away to the stairs at the rear of the hotel. Once Marshbrook was out of sight, the pretty, dark-haired receptionist turned her attention to the two Middle Eastern men, a smile on her face as she asked them if she could help. To Danny's surprise, one of the men pulled a silenced handgun from his jacket and shot the young woman in the forehead, the shocked look locked on her face as she toppled off the back of the reception chair. Without delay, the other man moved around the back of the reception desk and pushed the woman out of sight in the space under it. Danny crossed the road, his eyes locked on the two men as they headed out of sight up the stairs.

Shit, that went sour quickly.

Moving inside, Danny pulled his own silenced Glock from his jacket and headed to the stairs. The stairwell was old and small in the centuries-old building, giving no view up the centre from the bottom to top. Taking the steps as fast as he could go without making a sound, Danny moved up each floor, stopping to listen on the landing, and continuing up when he couldn't hear anyone. When he finally reached the top floor, he darted his head into the landing, taking a quick mental snapshot of the empty corridor before entering and heading towards room 18. As he got closer, he could see the door slightly ajar. Standing to one side, Danny moved his ear close to the gap and listened. He could hear voices, too faint to tell what they were saying, but he guessed they would be facing away from the door as they questioned Marshbrook. With his gun raised, Danny took a few deep breaths, tensing and relaxing his leg muscles, priming them for fast movement as he played out a surprise shock-and-awe attack in his mind.

One, two, three.

Danny burst through the door with astounding speed, his gun up and ready to shoot both men as they turned. His plans were scuppered when he saw both men facing him with their guns up. On his second step into the room, Danny planted his right leg on the wall beside him and kicked himself sideways through the en-suite door as a bullet whizzed past his ear, punching a neat hole through the hotel door behind him.

'Stop we need him alive,' shouted one the men to the other.

In the en-suite, Danny pulled himself into the large cast iron bath. Firing over the lip, he punched a neat line of holes in the direction of the Middle Eastern men through the tile, wood and plaster wall that separated the en-suite from the bedroom. He heard grunts of pain as he found his target, followed by a stream of bullets erupting back his way, showering him in bits of plaster and tiles before striking the side of the heavy cast iron bathtub with a deafening clang.

When the gunfire ceased, Danny could just about hear heavy breathing and grunts of pain above the ringing in his ears. Poking his head above the tub, he closed one eye and looked through a bullet hole into the bedroom. He could see one man face down on the bed, and the legs of someone on the floor. Climbing out of the tub, Danny spun out of the en-suite into the bedroom, his gun trained on the man sitting on the floor, his back propped up against the outside wall. He looked at Danny with defeated eyes, blood oozing from his chest. The gun was still in his hand, but he no longer had the strength to lift it.

Danny turned to Marshbrook sitting in the corner, a crimson flood covering his white shirt from his freshly opened-up neck. Flipping open Marshbrook's overnight bag, Danny found a Manila folder. He opened it to find details of the hotel booking and details of a job interview for an IT company in Paris. The name on the booking and interview was Jean Paul Marcellas. There was no information, no exchange. He'd been set up.

Danny folded the papers up and put them in his pocket before rifling through the pockets of the dead man on the bed. He went through the wallet. No ID, no cards, just some cash.

Crouching down in front of the man sitting against the wall, Danny slapped him lightly on the cheek.

'Who do you work for?' he said.

The man looked at him with semi-conscious eyes. His mouth was moving, but no sound was coming out. Without expression, Danny reached over, grabbed a pillow off the bed and shoved it over the man's face. He pushed the silencer of his gun into the middle of the pillow and pulled the trigger with a dull metallic ping. The man's body jerked before slumping back down. Throwing the pillow to one side, Danny removed the man's phone and some vehicle keys. He placed the man's thumb on the phone to unlock it and frowned when his own picture looked back at him. Pocketing the phone, Danny picked up the vehicle keys and stood. He noticed the Enterprise keyring on the keys and walked to the window. With a press of the button, Danny watched the hazard lights of the van below flash as it unlocked.

Feeling the need to get out, Danny took a neatly folded towel off the chair and went into the bathroom. He wiped down the cast iron bath and doors on the way out, taking the towel with him to avoid leaving any DNA. A minute later he was out of the hotel. He looked up and down the narrow road as he crossed to the Enterprise rental van. All was quiet, just the odd Parisian and tourist. Danny got into the van and started it up. He glanced in the back before pulling away, frowning at the sight of a crate with its lid off. The inside was lined with foam, and handcuffs and chains were fixed on the thick wooden sides. With the unnerving thought that someone wanted him kidnapped and crated, Danny pulled into the Paris traffic.

TWO

'Wait here,' she said, leaving her bodyguards in the foyer of The Savoy Hotel without waiting for an answer.

'Good evening, Miss Volkov,' said the maître d' of Kaspar's restaurant.

'Good evening, Samuel. You have my usual table ready?' she said, her voice polite but cold and unemotional, with a heavy Russian accent.

'Of course, and your guest is already here,' said Samuel, walking ahead of her to get her seated.

The heels of her Christian Louboutins tapped rhythmically as she followed. Heads turned as she passed through the restaurant in a figure-hugging designer dress, that complimented her long blonde hair and striking, ice-blue eyes.

James Bullman got up out of his seat to greet her as she approached. 'Annika, my dear, so good to see you,' he said, sitting back down as Samuel slid the chair in behind Annika as she sat.

'Can I get you something to drink?' said Samuel, handing them menus.

'Beluga vodka on the rocks,' said Annika, her eyes fixed on James.

'Eh, just tonic water for me, please. I've got Cabinet meetings this afternoon,' said James, his political face locked in its usual public smile.

As Samuel left, James looked back to Annika, her unwavering, ice-cold stare causing his smile to falter for a second before he composed himself.

'He got away,' she said as a blunt statement of

fact.

'Er, yes, I'm afraid he did.'

'What kind of imbeciles did you send?' said Annika, leaning in as she spoke angrily.

'They were highly trained assets. Look, I did as you asked. It's not my fault Pearson got away. Now, this is not the time or place to discuss it,' he said, his voice hushed and eyes flicking around nervously in case they were overheard.

'Do not dare to silence me, Mr Bullman. I may be young, but I am my father's daughter. He owned you. Now I own you,' said Annika, her voice returning to its calm and chilling tone.

'Now listen here, young lady. Whatever agreement your father and I had, it ended when he died. I arranged Paris out of respect for him, but that's it. No more,' said James, his face reddening at being spoken to by this young upstart.

'You know, Mr Bullman, when the trustees released my father's business affairs to me on my twenty-first birthday, I spent much time going through his journals and business effects.' Annika paused, her face expressionless as she stared unblinking at Bullman. His practiced political I hid his thoughts, but his eyes gave away his growing nerves.

'There is some very interesting video footage in there, some that would cause even the most broadminded members of your constituency to be shocked by your sexual preferences. A taste so niche I believe one of the women from the brothel ended up in hospital and still carries the scars,' said Annika, pausing once again to watch the colour drain from Bullman's face.

'I did not spend five years trying to find out who killed my father, to give up, Mr Bullman. The arrangements are made. All you have to do is deliver him. Daniel Pearson will suffer, and when I decide the time is right, he will beg me to kill him. Get it done, Mr Bullman. Do I make myself clear?'

'Perfectly. Now if you'll excuse me, I've rather lost my appetite,' said James, getting up to leave.

Samuel arrived with the drink as Bullman left. 'Is your guest not staying?' he asked.

'I'm afraid Mr Bullman had some pressing business to deal with, so I will be dining alone tonight,' Annika said, taking a sip of her Beluga vodka on the rocks.

'Very good, madam,' said Samuel, giving Annika a menu before clearing Mr Bullman's cutlery and glass away.

Buy Now

About the Author

Stephen Taylor was born in 1968 in
Walthamstow, London.

I've always had a love of action thriller
books, Lee Child's Jack Reacher and Vince
Flynn's Mitch Rapp and Tom Wood's Victor. I
also love action movies, Die Hard, Daniel
Craig's Bond and Jason Statham in The
Transporter and don't get me started on Guy

Richie's Lock Stock or Snatch. The harder and faster the action the better, with a bit of humour thrown in to move it along.

The Danny Pearson series can be read in any order. Fans of Lee Child's Jack Reacher or Vince Flynns Mitch Rapp and Clive Cussler or Mark Dawson novels will find these book infinitely more fun. If your expecting a Dan Brown or Ian Rankin you'll probably hate them.

Www.stephentaylorbooks.com

<u>The Danny Pearson Thriller Series</u>

Printed in Great Britain
by Amazon